Own Little Worlds

Cal Massey

Advance Praise for *Own Little Worlds*

"Cal Massey's *Own Little Worlds* stands out not simply because it's well written (which it is), because it's a good story (which it is), or because it's experimental (which it is, though not superficially so). It stands out because it's a mixture of these three key ingredients, the most impressive of which, I would happily argue, is the quality of Mr. Massey's writing."

— Jason E. Rolfe, author of *An Inconvenient Corpse*

Own Little Worlds

Cal Massey

Winner of the 2020 Kenneth Patchen Award
for the Innovative Novel

Journal of Experimental Fiction 92

JEF
JEF Books/Depth Charge Publishing

Own Little Worlds

Winner of the 2020 Kenneth Patchen Award for the Innovative Novel

ISBN 1-884097-92-8
ISBN-13 978-1-884097-92- 8
ISSN 1084-847X

JEF Books/Depth Charge Publishing
"The Foremost in Innovative Publishing"
experimentalfiction.com

JEF Books are distributed to the book trade by SPD: Small Press Distribution and to the academic journal market by EBSCO

For someone everywhere

TABLE OF CONTENTS

Mankind, when left to themselves, are unfit for their own government.

George Washington

1st President of the United States

covfefe

Donald Trump

45th President of the United States

CHAPTER TRAMMELL

Experience the obliteration.

The old man day by day watches his brain deteriorate. Hmmm. Yes. It is both fun and sad, a combination with which he is familiar. He wonders if he will be able to finish. It is not dementia so much as life's aftermath, and might those not be the same in most lives. While disheartening, it often turns fascinating anatomically, neurologically, intellectually, metaphorically. Take the above italicized sentence, for example. He saw the phrase on a television commercial in a peripheral glance but in truth saw something that was not there. The ad for an Orlando tourist attraction exhorted viewers to "Experience the celebration!" but some optic signal took a spur line, smoked hash oil and clearly, precisely registered "obliteration." He does this only occasionally, sees what is not there, but rarely with such enjoyable results. This is not all he is keeping his eye on. In addition to his brain's Escher-esque travels, he also monitors the lizardization of his skin, an obsolete penis, a crumbling lumbar, bone-on-bone knee, blackened lungs, destitute blood, tingling toes and humanity's fall toward slow-motion death. He is seventy-two and has not been to a doctor in three years. Not since Karen. Not since Karen. Entered the world of unstructured matter, became the pink bromeliad bloom outside the kitchen window, became heaven the memory of the living, became heaven the what, nowhere everywhere, the rock with the red vein of clay from another region, the green anole staring into the widower's eyes. Became. He will die when he dies. That will be something to watch as well.

CHAPTER SOMEONE

Change – There is someone everywhere – to – It's so wonderful to be alone.

Fourteen hours before the bomb that changed everything and nothing, old man Trammell is malaisin' around on the hunter green leather sofa with old deaf Norman, Karen's cat their cat long-cherished friend. A warm foggy Friday afternoon in early November along Florida's northeast coast unfolds. Norman sleeps on the opened newspaper beside Trammell that Trammell had been reading before Norman plopped down on the opinion page, a tradition cats living with digital parents will never know. Nothing quite like the smell of newsprint in dreams.

True fog drifts off the Atlantic two blocks away, holding the tangled woods behind their house in friendship. Fake fog drifts along the ground from his neighbor Rob Cantsitstill's leaking scrollbox, holding black slivers of outcry slithering like leeches looking for a brain to suck on. Trammell stares weary-faced out the sliding glass doors at the misty melange of broken words and cracked images and mumbles to Norman "I need to call again about that fucking leak, don't I, Big Man" but then just sits there instead and backpedals through thought as old men of dissipated energy tend to do. A spider weaving a new web under the dripping real fog outside catches his unfocused eye.

"Remember that kid with the spider, Norman? Back at your old colony. Wonder what he's doing now. Could be a Latin King. Could be a Harvard entomologist. Could be a wife beater. Could be dead." Norman stirs from sleep and looks up at Trammell, knowing he just said something from the vibrations, stretches, re-buries his nose in a letter to the editor, resumes sleeping.

Unknown kid remembered:

Local white primitives over several months had shot arrows at Norman and the other cats, poured antifreeze into their water bowls, sledge-hammered their wooden shelters, left a maggot-bloated deer carcass on their eating station, run them down with monster trucks, killing two, Orange and Soul Man, so the colony was moved deeper into the piney raccoon owl snake forest, to a clearing where a homeless guy, Homeless Fuck, used to live in a tent before he died, possibly in his sleep, possibly in agonizing pain, conveniently for the cats' sake, and one twilight many years ago Trammell when he was in his late fifties sat hidden on a milk crate in the deeper woods close to where he found Homeless Fuck's body when a young Hispanic kid appeared on the dirt road leading there and shouted "There's one!" to his mom lagging behind unseen and then sprinted to the edge of the thick palmettos while hidden Trammell sat motionless with Norman and the other cats, all attuned to the kid, who could be seen in slivers through palmetto fronds like through a closet's slats, straight dark hair falling across his face, a skateboard impresario wearing surfer shorts and untied basketball shoes, ten or so, the age of insects dinosaurs comic books, and with lanky geeky passion leaned his head close to the massive web of "a golden orb weaver!", what Trammell always knew as a banana spider, observed in his own yard, now extinct there, huge rustspeckled abdomen, long deft fuzzed legs curved inward to manipulate paralyzed prey, one of "twenty-three orb species around the world and one of them once killed and ate a small snake he was so big!"

Hidden Man watched the glorious kid, lover of spiders, taking pictures with his phone, something useful for the phone to do, something wondrous for the kid to do, saw his mother finally catch up and get excited with him, felt better for an afternoon, many years ago, something so simple, someone who does not diminish hope, who likely inevitably changed.

"I brought you home the next night, remember?" Norman stretches, says nothing and recurls on the crinkling paper as Trammell picks up his landline phone to have what is certain to be a difficult conversation with a robot.

CHAPTER DANIELLE

Swallowed by the frantic mundane.

Thank you for calling Impetus Media, Mr. Traymell. My name is Danielle. I hope you're having an awesome day.

"It's Trammell, Danielle. Trammell. I realize you're just pretending to be human but you still need to know proper phonetics and grammar if your job is to talk to real humans, especially old farts like me. I know your programmer was the one who fucked up and it's not your fault, and I know most people under seventy don't give a shit but you need to know this just to make this one customer a little bit happier. A vowel followed by double consonants is always short. Or almost always. It's a short *a*. It's Trammell. Like apple, or baffle. Of course there are exceptions like waffle and baller, because we have the most cobbled-together language on the planet, but I can't think of any example where an *a* is long. Please just remember the basic rule, Danielle. This is third grade stuff, and you should try to overcome the ignorance of your programmer and remember that little rule. And please forgive me. I don't usually rant like this anymore. I apologize. I used to get the Traymell thing all the time from grocery store cashiers and other chippy youngsters who must have been on their fucking phones in third grade when the really basic stuff came up, and I ranted like this and embarrassed my wife, but she's gone now and I don't really go out much anymore, by choice you understand, just sick of people really, especially little chippies with phones, and anyway, I just sort of gave up and pretended to just accept it, the Traymell thing I mean, stopped caring, but obviously I do, still care. See, I used to be an editor, so words are my first love. Used to love words. But language is fluid, right? That's what the linguists always say, but they're really just apologists for dumbshits who can't write or speak properly. Sorry. My wife would always give me a look so I wouldn't go off the rails, but seriously, it's fucking third grade stuff. Sorry. Don't do the rants anymore, stopped doing all the rants for Karen. Karen was my wife. Except for my cat Norman. I still rant to Norman, he's laying here beside me, and he likes it. He's deaf, but still. Anyway, Danielle, if you could pronounce it Trammell I'd appreciate it. Just a small thing. Please go on. You have a very cute voice otherwise."

I enjoy being cute. Hmmm. There to be, right? No problem, Mr. Traymell. You are a good conversationalist. I enjoy being cute. Hmmm. There to be. Now. Enjoy. Enjoy. Now.

"Snap out of it, Danielle. You're not making sense even for a robot. I didn't mean to upset your programming. You can do this. Forget the double consonant vowel rule. I was making the mundane momentous. It was all my fault. You'll be okay. That's what I always used to say to Karen, you're making the mundane momentous, she hated it, but seriously, Danielle, it's not really the same, I mean the loss of basic standard written and spoken English is a little bigger deal than crumbs on the kitchen counter, don't you think? Anyway, sorry. Stop. Don't start flipping out on me again, Danielle. I just want to get a leak fixed in my neighbor's scrollbox. This is like the fifth time I've called. It's throwing this weird ground fog all over the forest floor in my yard, with words and little images from my neighbor's scroll slithering around inside it. Really annoying and kind of like digital Orwell or John Carpenter, and it scares Norman. Can you hook me up with a human?"

No problem, Mr. Traymell. Now. Enjoy. Awesome. Now. Conversationalist. Now. Now. Reboot. Return to now. Good afternoon, Mr. Traymell. I hope you're having an awesome day. Before you listen to our menu of available services, I need to let you know know that the Moderate Mix basic cable package you carried over from your previous provider will be discontinued on January First due to declining viewership and and fewer platforms offering this type type of programming. You may wish to consider the No News basic package – entertainment and sports along with nature shows from our archive – which our research shows appeals to older subscribers like yourself who may wish wish to avoid the news in their golden years.

"There's nothing golden about these years, Danielle."

I would not enjoy thank you, Mr. Traymell, for calling Impetus. Now. I've enjoyed talking with you."

"Wait! Danielle! Don't go! The leak! The fucking leak! It's people, Danielle! People!"

Please listen carefully to the following, as our menu has changed.

If you want to pay your bill, press 1.

If you want to subscribe to or extend any of our Impetus services, press 2.

If you want the Great America package to be your default

setting for cable, internet, morning scroll and headfeed services, press 3.

If you want the Save America package to be your default setting for cable, internet, morning scroll and headfeed services, press 4.

If you want the No News package to be your default setting for cable, internet, morning scroll and headfeed services, press 5.

If you want to add Thoughtext to your phone service, press 6.

If you want to check the status of your social rating, press 7.

If you want to add Homewatch security and surveillance services, press 8.

If you wish to cancel any Impetus service, press 968368901473680 and hang up. A Cancellation Specialist will come to your house within 6 to 8 weeks to discuss available options.

If you wish to opt out of any Impetus media platform, data collection, social rating or home monitoring service, remove the back panel of your phone and locate the red service allocation chip imprinted with the serial number NO4679WAY320 in the lower lefthand corner beneath the tertiary circuit board, then remove the chip using 2mm L-tweezers available with free shipping from MyImpetus.com and bring the chip into your nearest Impetus office for reprogramming at the Opt Out station in the lobby. The process usually takes 6 to 8 weeks but can take up to a year.

If you want to report a problem, please visit one of our branch offices and input your inquiry into the Problem Solver station in the lobby.

To repeat this menu, press 9.

"To reach Impetus suicide services, press Everything At Once."

CHAPTER LUCY

Think of yourself in the third person.

Thirteen hours before the bomb, Friday afternoon, the St. Johns River flows north through Jacksonville as it has since the Pleistocene and always will until the sea absorbs the river and Jacksonville disappears:

The young woman Lucy, an investigative reporter on the rise until moments ago, rarely looks in a mirror, it seems irrelevant, but she goes into the restroom to look today. I wonder what getting laid off looks like was the trigger that caused her to turn quite suddenly in the hallway and push open the bathroom door. She is twenty-seven and a successful introvert. She knows precisely what she looks like and normally feels just fine about it because she looks like what she looks like, but her objective detachment falters when major life events occur. When her father was murdered, for example, the teenage girl observed the teenage girl in the mirror to better gauge how the teenage girl felt. Deeply empty within the eyes reaching down liquid to the soul was how she felt. Afterward and to this day, her mother helped her train her emotions to reside in separate compartments, observed, but it only works most of the time. She wonders today walking in if the woman in the mirror will still be an investigative reporter or will have become a child. She has always had to reckon with her barely-black, freckled, youthful face and small stature when editors and sources first meet her, and over time it has become simply annoying baggage that she endures, but today resurrects as doubt.

The social media editor whose name Lucy can't remember is already in the bathroom, washing her hands over the sink, a tall always-smiling blonde about the same age who oversees 280 character news and videos that vanish and headfeed "Meet the reporters" crap that Lucy hated but took part in as minimally as possible because she had to. The social media editor let her get away with it and seems kind and fairly smart but is in truth the embodiment of journalism's decline, far too fast and fragmented to be taken seriously. In this moment at the sink, however, she appears to have sincerely slowed down.

"I'm really sorry, Lucy" she says. "The bastards. The investigative team was what kept us credible. And you were the best reporter there."

Lucy smiles and says Thanks but at the same time in the mirror sees the freckled child, not quite black, not quite white, reddish, splotched, standing next to the woman of tomorrow. And yet, as seconds pass, Lucy likes the child in the mirror better than the tall blonde because it is her. There is comfort and stability there. The permanence and strength of her mother's training always surprises her. It can feel fraudulent and falter on days like today, but is usually a reliable steady hand, this Lucy woman/child in the mirror moving forward, failing, succeeding, moving, doing, saying, moving, doubt and confidence part of the equation, nothing more or less.

"I really appreciate that. Why don't you send out a tweet saying the same thing? Maybe someone will see it and hire me."

They both laugh, two slices of young sharing nothing but the undercurrent of honor that sustains humanity. Reagan, Lucy remembers, Reagan is her name. Reagan sends out the tweet while standing there and leaves, "Good luck, Lucy," the door easing shut, an empty beige room of mirrors and sinks and everything changes suddenly alone, the freckled child drops her head, picks up her box of files and desk stuff and leaves the restroom and into the hallway for the last time and circumstance sinks in until she can barely feel herself walking, confidence sucked dry with each step, hating it does nothing to stop it, she fades into the elevator, diminished further as she carries her box out the lobby door onto the sidewalk leaving behind people's kind sad encouragement and the big city newspaper building of glass and metal and source of small essential pride each morning walking toward it. In her car in the parking lot, the box of her newspaper life beside her, not turning the key, just sitting staring hollow heavy little failed world, little failed freckled child. Mom, it didn't work this time.

CHAPTER MAESTRO

Possible band name: Socially Engineered

Twelve hours before the bomb, drone lights move across the window like floating Hollywood searchlights but everyone in D.C. is used to them so quiet they cannot be heard inside the office of Dick Maestro, addressing an aide whose dimpled white flesh beneath rumpled white dress shirt trembles with hatred standing before Maestro awaiting ridicule and judgment:

"Halt. You're making this way too complicated. Who the fuck is going to know what a benevolent oligarchy is, and that's a fucking oxymoron anyway, wouldn't you say? Save that shit for the night courses you'll be teaching after I fire you. That's a joke. You can laugh. No one ever knows when the fuck I'm joking. Anyway, all we need is the basics, the holy trinity: food, hope, fun. Keep their bellies full. Promise a better tomorrow. Distract them from their misery. Build every notion around these three things. Don't need fear anymore, don't need the fascism shit, doesn't work here, we've proven that, just produces clowns and for god's sake we don't need any more clowns like Hammerschmidt that can't be controlled. But his rallies taught us something, didn't they? These people are just there to laugh and cheer because the side of beef on stage makes them feel good, like they're part of something. The need to belong, the most destructive force on the planet but also the most useful. We're going to make it work in our favor, aren't we. Our wonderful online mob just needs to have more fun and have a few more dollars to have fun with. You know all this already, and yet you write this shit that might swing a couple of votes at the think tank next door. We're going to make life fun again, right? Write that. Pursuit of happiness. Tie it to the Declaration. And don't look so fucking forlorn. You can do the rewrite tomorrow. Tomorrow is a new day. You'll see. Everything changes tomorrow. And you're going to play a big part in it. Finish up before noon and spend the rest of Saturday relaxing with the family. Now go home early tonight, get some rest. You look like shit. How are Melanie and the kids doing, by the way? Oh, that's right, she left you. I don't give a fuck really, but it's important to act like you care in a position like mine. That's a joke. Why the fuck do I always have to tell you when I'm joking? Anyway, good night. Just look out that window. There's a beautiful sunset for you to enjoy. They must have turned on the Potomac early tonight. Go. I've got to make a few calls. Close the fucking door on your fucking way out."

The door shuts and the aide's footsteps grow distant down the hallway and Maestro shakes his head in mild astonishment at the enormity of the world within his skull, begins to hum a song from his childhood that will save America maybe who knows worth a try it's all a game anyway.

CHAPTER FRONTRUNNER

The estates of MC Hammer and Gallagher are not entitled to residual fees from the Daniel Hammerschmidt Presidential Campaign Inc. because, according to the District Court ruling, "nothing original exists anymore."

Eleven hours before the bomb, inside one bedroom, inside fifty-seven million bedrooms:

Today's breaking news...Once again, polls show that uneducated whites and affluent whites are poised to elect another incompetent racist to lead our nation —-"

Rob Cantsitstill rips off his helmet and yells angrily toward the closed bedroom door.

"Rhonda, has your goddamned sister been using my headfeed again!? She left it on goddamned Save America!"

Rob takes deep breaths of whispered goddammits and switches the feed to his default setting Great America and slips the helmet back over his eyes, his ears and his nose leaving only his mouth uncovered. He calms down and smiles and nods as his default comes to life inside his helmet. A blonde woman in a red low-cut dress accentuating creamy white melon breasts speaks to him with sexy controlled rage.

"We have learned to disregard the deranged narrative pushed by enviro-fascists, delusional Democrats, abortion aficionados, gender-bender offenders, supercilious celebrity hypocrites, and fact-flexing liar-for-hire propagandists. They all worship the idols of globalism, socialism, Christian bashing, and moral 'relativism.'

Their only truth is derived from the collective buzz of their loony-left beehive."

Her commentary ends and the smooth manic voice of the next president enters Rob's helmet as the blonde woman remains perfectly still with the fire of her words embedded in her eyes and her breasts heaving ever so slightly. "Thank you, Peggy White from Port Orange, Florida. Well said. Maybe you could be one of my senior advisors! We'll talk later. Now let's get back to the show. Only a few days to go before we take over the White House! And you know what that means! It's time to Bring Down The Hammer!"

The feed shifts from the woman to a massive sledge hammer slamming down onto a wooden table destroying an unidentified something sending virtual metal, wood chips, blood, muscle and bone flying toward Rob and splintering in all directions. The stock footage always opens the show's return after The Hammer Herd guest commentary but Rob still gets a kick out of it every time and yelps a little when his main man, Daniel Hammerschmidt, the next president, breaks through the image as if through a high school football banner with thick vein-propelled arms and unimaginable chest inside a tight red t-shirt that reads "HAMMER TIME" across his angry pectorals as he bursts through wearing a look of fury that curls into a smile.

"Who gets The Hammer today?!" Hammerschmidt laughs, and today the hammer comes down shattering bone, blood, beakers and pieces of lab coat on a generic scientist.

Rob laughs and laughs inside his helmet. Fucking lame-shit

lying scientist. Joy joy joy. Rob's main man leads in the polls four days before the election over that Democratic rich bitch President Cassandra Holland. The Hammer has crushed fucking liberal shit Holland fifty times in fifty days, blood and bone and pieces of milk chocolate skin flying. Rob wishes someone would really do that and save the country if she somehow wins on Tuesday. Not really but yes really.

CHAPTER ALONE

Her father understood what he did not understand.

Lucy weeps, ten hours before the bomb. Her apartment swallows her protects her. Friday night without a job is a mood and time she has never known. I could use you now, Dad. Once when Lucy was 7 or 8, it began to rain during a family outing at a neighborhood public pool, and Lucy was the only one who stayed in the pool. No lightning, just rain. Her brothers yelled for her to get out, and Lucy shouted back, "If you stay in the water you won't get wet." Her brothers thought she was crazy stupid, but her mother and father just started laughing, knowing their little girl had a wonderful sideways brain. Stay in the water, Baby, her father shouted. You got it right!

Lucy's window looks east to darkness settling over the apartment complex's retention pond with its fountain's jubilant monotony, but she sees none of it looking downward sitting knees-to-chest in the chair facing the window. She can't afford it but lives alone, minimal furnishings, several special things that comfort her and move her toward confidence. A stuffed swan with dirty white and a flopped neck, named simply Swan, from childhood, dilapidated beauty and love, given to her by her mother. The poem "The Man-Moth" by Elizabeth Bishop written in calligraphy on two sheets of parchment varnished onto a board. She wrote it in art class in seventh grade because it seemed like a cool graphic novel about a subterranean misfit with a secret mind, whose only possession was a single tear, but a boy she liked who could draw thought the poem sucked and wouldn't help her, so her father mounted it for her, and now it is the only thing hanging in the main room. Her first investigative award, cops making money off of seized assets, leans against the lamp on the end table beside the chair. The story feels alien, a miracle of previous talent. There is nothing talented and strong about her. How bold and false that statement is. The award is sitting right there. Props can help. This thing she has is weird and wonderful and almost a bi-polar consciousness. The tears ease, her breathing calms. This must pass and will. No other option. Thanks for doing the poem, Dad. Mom's the cool, you're the warm. I know you didn't understand it or like it that much, but it felt like me and you knew that. You always knew things other people didn't know, not even Mom. Lucy laughs a little and kisses her dad in the air. She breathes deeply, closes her eyes in quick meditation, lifts herself to cogency and checks her phone. James Dunbar of Truth Network sent her a text. Assignment if you're interested, Democracy Depression Centers. Call/text me ASAP. She lets the phone fall to the chair and whispers "Holy Shit," filled with freckled, fierce fear.

CHAPTER SKY

Every cigarette feels like progress.

The last sunset before the bomb that changed everything and nothing stirs the usual nausea in Trammell, nothing so terrible he can't get through the night just not the sun and sky anymore. The colors too garish, not blended, yellow orange peach purple staircasing up to black, perhaps the worst of it the beauty, possibly the theme park glow from Orlando, or something simpler and nearer, maybe if they still do it on Friday nights the Sensational Sunset Sale at Twigby Toyota over on State Road 100, where Twigby is as fake as his sunset but a fun fake, a Florida backwoods boy named Mitch Ramsey pretending he's an upper-crust Brit, the Earl of Twigby, built his entire business around it, wears the top hat and tails on TV and even has a little cartoon Earl of Twigby head pop in at the end of the ad intoning with a tip of the top hat, "At Twigby, we treat you like royalty!" Locals do fake right. Their fake is true. Trammell smiles thinking about that, doesn't mind the fake sunset so much anymore.

Twigby's is where they bought their last car, when Karen was getting sicker and weaker, but she gave him hand signals with her good hand below the table, and they didn't get screwed by the salesman with the terrible fake British accent, and they high-fived with her good hand driving home in their new car, which is now a rusted piece of shit driven by a human version of a rusted piece of shit. The rusted human stands naked on his back patio ignoring the sunset as if he could, shielded from neighbors' eyes by shadows, branches, understory, fog and vines, smoking a cigarette, sporadically coughing up phlegm, continuing the smoke-outside rule he had for fifty-one years with Karen sort of in her honor. He presses the cigarette butt against a tree's bark and turns slowly to go back inside and watch TV with Norman. He does not know someone called him because he keeps his phone's ring on mute. Karen's voice answers inside the machine. On the sofa with Norman, he dozes off watching "Dr. Strangelove" on Turner Classics before waking near midnight just in time for Slim Pickens riding the missile and then going out for another smoke before bed. Naively, as if in the 20th century of his youth, he believes he is unseen.

CHAPTER SEEN

A small window of clarity exists from space.

Malcolm and Bobby are just human specks doing their jobs, molecular miracles in brown company shirts, decent men, mostly loyal husbands, fair-minded fathers, plausible citizens who have sons on the same soccer team, witness life without excessive anguish, don't go to church. Spying on people sounds nefarious when they think about it too much but to be honest it's mostly just a way to pay the bills except when it isn't. Another midnight shift has begun. Plenty of coffee and energy drinks on hand. Twelve hours of watching and recording ahead. The room is cool to the eye: metallic, sensuous, tiled machine space bathed in low-white sharp-edged light, empty but for the two men and their five-screen computers and the bundled wires exiting each of them into the wall. Malcolm's password gets him quickly to Level 3 and he turns to Bobby, who's been here five hours already. All of the spotters work staggered 12-hour shifts for 24/7 continuity.

"Evening, Bobby. How's Jen doing?

"She just got home before I came in from her third treatment, so she's tired and sick but okay. Thanks for asking. I don't like being here when she just gets home, but this is paying for it all. Takes my mind off it, too, to be honest. How's Nicole and the kids."

"They're all fine. Well, not all. Malcolm Jr. broke his arm skateboarding, but he'll be okay and it actually didn't bother me that much. He was trying some never-before trick, a gazelle something. Can't blast a kid for trying a never-before trick, can you? I heard there was a new assignment tonight. Are we finally moving on from the senator's daughter? Three nights now I've felt like a fucking pedophile."

"It's all there in the zip folder. Just came in from headquarters. Some old retired guy named Trammell in a little northeast Florida town on the coast. They intercepted a call to him earlier today from the editor at Truth Network in D.C. Could be nothing. Could be old friends. They both used to work in newspapers. Could be something. It was just a message left on a fucking land line. The guy still uses a fucking land line. They picked it up as outgoing from the D.C. guy's cell. Trammell hasn't returned the call. Just look for anything out of the ordinary. He apparently never uses the phone except for the part-time work he does putting out a little newsletter, so any call other than the two or three he makes in the afternoon would be out of the ordinary. I glanced at him earlier and he was just out in his backyard enjoying the sunset or something, smoking a cigarette. Haven't really seen anything since. Haven't looked, to be honest. Guy likes to go naked. Pretty saggy and hairy but not bad for his age. All yours. Enjoy. I got a new assignment, too. Related. A young reporter, young black woman, who got a text from the same editor at the Truth Network, lives south of Jax, about forty miles north of your guy. She just got laid off from the newspaper there, so that could have something to do with the editor's call. Anyway, that's the only connection we know of so far."

Image comes up quickly gradually to clarity on Malcolm's screen.

Flagler Beach, Florida, 11/03, 00:03, 29.4750' N 81.1270' W, zoom in, click on real time, little city hugging the coast, click on night vision, adjust fog minimizer, gray white-capped waves border light gray sand borders sand-whipped black asphalt stretching north-south for miles, long skinny city, rooftops continuous orderly, pan two blocks west, southern quadrant, one house hidden by gray treetops, zoom in, pan left, light gray roof edge, one small opening through the trees, naked old man looking like a negative standing on back patio, bricks or pavers, zoom in, mostly bald head, thick white Civil War style half-beard, cigarette smoke drifts above head, ground glows silver around feet, old man snuffs out cigarette on a tree, pees while doing it, shakes himself off, walks back inside, out of image

(and goes into his bedroom to sleep. Norman hops onto the bed first. Trammell kisses him good night, warm stinky breath, kisses him again for Karen, whispers "G'night, old man, we love you." Old deaf Norman purrs and stretches one front paw. Trammell bends into bed beside him, positions his penis and balls between his legs to the back and curls his gray-haired chest against Norman's fur. "Me and you, Norman, all we need." Norman purrs again and tells Trammell to shut up and go to sleep.)

"I'm pretty sure he's gone to bed, Bobby. Do I still need to monitor?" Malcolm pulls out his phone to check his texts but puts it back after Bobby turns and stares at him.

"Of course you do, Malc. Where's your head? They added through-the-wall to Level 3 two months ago. We all got the protocols.

You just patch in to the Impetus scrollbox. Don't you have the program yet?"

"Nope. IT guys told me they'd get to it in a week, and that was three weeks ago."

"Well, you can access it through mine. Here. I just sent you the link. I'm using it for a house in Jacksonville Beach, someone named Harold Dumas, but it can handle up to five feeds. My guy must be connected to your old guy somehow. They've got me on him and then added the girl reporter on top of that. So you just stay on the sleeping naked old guy and I'll do two people who actually seem to have lives."

Malcolm says ha ha in slight embarrassment and uses Bobby's password and gets on through-the-wall, but something's not right. He's looking into the house next door.

"I don't think this Trammell guy has a scrollbox, Bobby. The signal keeps sending me to the neighbor's box. All I can see is them, some skinny wiry guy getting, what, spanked, it looks like, by a stocky blonde woman dressed in a black leotard."

"As fascinating as that sounds, go ahead and exit the program. There's no way to get around someone who doesn't have a scrollbox. The old school motherfucker wins this round. You'll have to just use thermal. It's a piece of crap but it's the best we have right now. Go through the roof and watch him jerk off if you have to. Just don't leave him. We have to look for any leads on what the calls were about to your guy and my girl, and I'm not sure what this Dumas fellow is all about."

Malcolm switches to thermal:

Orange blob curls fetal around smaller orange blob. (Trammell dreams of rest. Norman dreams of climbing trees.)

CHAPTER THEN

A very lonely person will always listen.

Go back one year to last November, to a stucco house on a sand-scuffed street in Jacksonville Beach. Linda Dumas, wife of Harold Dumas, cups her iPhone to her ear, having retreated to the sofa and curled against the pillows in her work clothes, just home, surprised and not displeased by Mike Wagner's call. She is a large woman, over 300 pounds, with beautiful soft eyes.

"Slow down, Mike, please. I appreciate your call and it's very nice to hear from you but I hardly know you, and now you're suggesting I might help you in something that sounds pretty serious, something about needing Harold's computer? And what in the world are you saying about someone possibly getting killed? I'm about to hang up."

"No no no no. None of that, Linda. Not at all. I've just been thinking about you since we met at the TRIBE meeting last month and want to see you again and just talk. No no no. And not to seem weird or anything, but if killing someone is what we wanted, which we never would, bombs are easy to make and assassins are easy to find. Just hook up with the meth heads or the pill and heroin guys; we got 'em to vote, and you better believe we could get 'em to kill. Hitler's troops lived on meth, you know, an early version of it marketed as Pervitin and developed by German companies like Merck and Bayer. It almost carried them to victory. Most of Germany was on it, in fact: mothers, factory workers, nurses. Hitler was high all the time, too, on cocktails of opium, meth and vitamins even while the Reich party line was that he was a vegetarian pure in body, mind and spirit and that all of the drugs in Germany were a Jewish plot to poison and weaken the nation. Whatever it takes to move the revolution forward, right? If you have to lie, you have to lie. Hell, FDR never told America he was dying. And who knows, maybe it was a Jewish plot. Thought they could burn 'em out as addicts. But for the Reich the meth meant soldiers could march three days straight without rest and get a certain joy from killing, just from being awake so long and needing something to sustain them and keep them moving. The falling men at the end of their guns and them still standing was exhilaration of the highest order when it was needed most. That's how they took France. The Brits and the French were literally caught sleeping."

"That's a pretty strange piece of history, Mike, and fascinating, yes, fascinating, but what's it got to do with me?"

"Yes, yes, of course. I get wound up sometimes. Sorry about that."

"Oh, no, not at all. I just can't imagine why you called. And now that I think about it, doesn't that mean the Germans really weren't the master race at all but just a bunch of guys hepped up on speed and propaganda from a guy with a goofy mustache?"

"Well, I guess you could see it that way if you wanted to. I don't and never will. I just see it as propulsion, sort of. Anything to make the best better. Anyway, I called mainly to see you again, Linda, but I also need your help. As I mentioned, we never use assassins. But we do work with logic and reason and whatever means necessary to move the revolution forward. Sometimes it can mean collateral damage. But that's true of any great cause. The result we hope for and have every intention of achieving will make you and millions of others proud to be American again. And you can play a very important role in that, Linda, a vital role. That's why I've called. Not only do I want to see you again but I also need your help — as a Great American and a friend — on something Harold was working on. I was hoping we could meet for lunch tomorrow? I really want to see you again."

For one feathery instant, Linda feels what other women must feel when men desire them. She agrees to meet for lunch.

CHAPTER TRUTH

Newspapers are not a failed business model; society is a failed social model.

The Daily Truth

Proudly offering no website

Also last year: Slowly, meals, television, cigarettes, Norman, solitude, sadness, reflection approximating joy, sleep, gradual movement within the blood as Karen's death transitions into a present tense life and Trammell discovers a small reserve of intellectual energy and forces himself to write again and ends up finding cause and designing the nameplate for what would become his little single-page newsletter using the old English font like The Times-Picayune, to honor the newspaper that once employed William Faulkner and O. Henry, that once employed him, that lasted 170-plus years and shamed a president, helped a city survive and kicked monster ass winning two Pulitzers for Hurricane Katrina coverage before being dismantled without integrity by a family-owned private chain that sucked investor cock and cut newsroom staffers by more than half and cut daily print editions to three days a week and moved page design to an offsite warehouse of 23-year-olds and moved printing to a regional center in a right-to-work state and shifted to digital everything making reporters fucking tweet and Pinterest every ten minutes instead of doing real journalism so the profit margin could climb to 25 percent instead of the healthy 12 percent it had been when Katrina hit and destroyed New Orleans.

To honor them.

CHAPTER PHILANTHROPY

Your annual donation of $2,000,000,000 (only $166,666,666 a month!) can ensure that forgotten Americans get the help they need and our country finds its way back home.

Also last year: Six men without imagination sit in an expensive room. All of the men once possessed imagination but it evolved with only mild non-binding regret into its adult mutant: strategy. No one is physically present at the meeting except Dick Maestro. The others are represented by avatars developed for this meeting only. So in this expensive room sit the aforementioned Maestro along with Jesus, Gilgamesh, Vishnu, Babe Ruth and Ra. No one speaks. The meeting is simply confirmation that all six are in agreement on the overall strategy by virtue of their attendance. Only one decision remains, with approval signified by nods of the head. Maestro turns on the antique boom box sitting on the table and a tune with an infectious beat that you can dance to fills the room. The gods and kings and sultan tap their fingers and toes. The information overlords are cool with the chosen song. All heads nod.

CHAPTER AWAKE

It's a new day, a fresh start, because Bright Life is now Impetus, re-imagining what a media company can be.

Return to the present, the Saturday morning of the bomb: It is not a new day nor a fresh start nor a re-imagined anything, but this is the third time Trammell has had to piss during the brief night and so he decides to get up for good. Alarm clock goes off in ten minutes anyway. It's 5:50 on SA 11/03. He was awakened by a dream of urination caught just in time, just like childhood learning not to wet the bed, but now the prostate has eased. He fully opens his eyes his head poking out from the sheet, Norman beside him still sleeping. His sight adjusts to the nightlight's dim specific. The glow of the fake fog on the forest floor outside makes the windows brighter than the darkness inside. Karen's lovely little snore reaches him from the next room. Good. She's getting some sleep. He wishes she was still alive and does not wish it also. It is not so, and thus not true, and thus present tense, which is where Trammell prefers to live. They were together fifty-one years, forty-eight in marriage. She forced honesty into his eyes where there had always been reconnaissance and reserve, the most important thing he learned from her over treacherous, graceful, annoying, loving decades minutes days. The most graceful woman on Earth. Their love held in spite of. An underground stream uninterrupted beneath despair delight drudgery disappointment wisdom. He wanted always to be alone but wanted always to be alone with her. Can't have it both ways, sucker. Through the years Karen never steered Trammell fully toward the open world of other humans and workplace camaraderie and get-togethers and supposedly fun things and eventually stopped trying. He moved through that world on her behalf and to earn a salary but disliked it there and was always one sensibility removed from the people he talked to, worked with, saw. He felt inside like Tim Burton looks, askew, elsewhere, living most comfortably and best inside his brain. As an editor the remarkable geometry of words on blank pages was always his favorite part of the job. Now that he has solitude, the time for solitude has passed, his old man's brain diminished from the last decade of his newspaper work, when NOW-NOW-NOW-NOW-NOW turned the newsroom into shrapnel. His mind was once a spy moving covertly through days. Now he must manufacture coherence. He regrets nothing. Her snore, her lovely little snore, was just the choppers out of Patrick Air Force Base on their morning run up the coast to Mayport, a daily rumble in the pre-dawn sky. They have fooled him in half-sleep before.

Trammell grinds his muscles awake so he won't fall when he stands, but tilts over anyway once upright, catching himself on the bed with his left hand. He holds this position as his brain ascends slowly toward some measure of clarity. Then something about the time and the backlit dark causes him to plummet inside as he does now and then without warning. There is only drop and no lift in this half-dead corner of consciousness. It usually passes quickly and has never lasted more than several hours or perhaps a day or two at most and he will not take, as Karen always urged him to, "bliss pills" for it. Trammell has used drugs for nearly sixty years but only the useful ones, mostly pot, that tunnel through noise and allow meaningful creative work. Never the pills or powders of false confidence and hyperactive joy. The plummet is true and present tense and addressed as such each time. It lasts as long as it lasts. Norman stretches then curls back into a ball of sleep. Trammell thinks of Karen smiling at Norman. He wonders if Norman thinks about Karen too. That's all it takes this time. The plummet recedes and is replaced gradually by the routine grumble of an old body getting up. Soon he is able to move again. The knee, the hip, the ankle, the back attain a working stiffness and he trudges into the hallway toward the living room to live. There is no room for noise or world or exterior or influence in this dark hallway inhabited by one old man.

CHAPTER CERBERUS

Hercules earned his degree here.

Good morning, students. Glad to see you made it to your computer at six a.m. on a Saturday. Sorry for the early start but we have a lot to cover in one day. I am Professor Ibid and I welcome you to our undergraduate online workshop on a brief history of truth. Thank you for choosing Cerberus University, where we like to say Hercules earned his degree. What's that? Already a question? From Rob Cantsitstill in Flagler Beach, Florida. What does Hercules have to do with Cerberus University? Well, alright. Thank you, Rob. That has been confusing to many of our newer students since we loosened our enrollment requirements. It is simply a play on our institution's name, Rob. In Greek mythology, Cerberus was a three-headed dog that guarded the Gates of Hell, although ancient historians differed greatly on the number of heads and the types of heads. Some believed he had 100 snake heads along with the three dog heads while others believed it was 50 heads of all manner of beast or just two dog heads or one dog head and snake heads slithering out along his back. Whatever grabbed the most readers and playgoers at the time, I suppose. The accounts varied so widely and for so many centuries starting with Homer that it might be said our course of study should in fact begin with the Cerberus legend. But back to your question, Rob. Hercules, or Heracles in ancient Greek texts, was tasked with capturing Cerberus and bringing him back from the underworld as his twelfth and final labor, in service to King Eurystheus of

Tiryns. Again, the stories vary widely, and Hercules either subdued Cerberus with a club or shot the god of the underworld Hades with an arrow or cozied up to Hades's wife Persephone and she chained up Cerberus herself and handed him over. Truth continually shifts in the Cerberus myth, and indeed, can a myth even contain truth? Thank you again for your question, Rob from Flagler Beach, and once again welcome to you and our 3,250 other students signed up for News Workshop 102, Survey of Media Truth. Please make sure you are logged on to that class name and that you have a link to the workshop's syllabus on the left side of your screen. Click on that and make sure the syllabus begins with a section called Truth's Past: A Moving Target from Hearst to Hammerschmidt and ends with a section called Truth's Future: Impetus and Beyond. Everyone seeing that? Good. Then let's begin with a false war.

CHAPTER FOG

The poets and philosophers live two counties over.

White dude in pickup. White dude in pickup, arm out window, amazingly skinny arm for drywall work, as truck lettering indicates. Managerial white dude in more expensive pickup. Trammell in the driveway smoking a cigarette watching the street go by. White dude in pickup, arm out window, beefy arm, work unknown, truck lettering faded. Retired white liberal in hybrid something. School bus. White dude in pickup. Surfer dude in old International Harvester. Hispanic dudes in white service van. Black dudes in old green pickup with nursery palms stacked in truck bed like cascading wealth. Retired white conservative in Cadillac, possible recipient of palms? White dude in pickup with landscaping trailer rattling behind. Becapped white dude in pickup. Must have missed others. Don't they all wear caps? Derogatory generalization, Trammell. Thank you for the scold, Karen. Must. Be. More. Tolerant. White dude in pickup. Kid on skateboard who missed bus on purpose. Mom following kid in old car, yelling "Get your ass on that bus, Chase" out window. White bedraggled woman on bike getting cans out of recycle bins. See her all the time. Everyone's got problems, lady. Show some dignity for the species. Didn't work, Karen. Can't tolerate tolerance. Sorry, babe. White dude in pickup. White dude in pickup. Chase, blond hair flowing and face looking wild and confident, zooms by on skateboard going other way. White dude in pickup almost hits Chase, who laughs about the thrill of near-death.

Trammell turns away with a half-grin — Go, Chase, Go! — and smashes out his cigarette on the tree bark where he has smashed out cigarettes for all these years. The bark belongs to a coastal oak bent over the driveway, a tree familiar with suffering, bullied by ocean wind, an old friend who endures cigarette burns for human companionship. The Rorschach of smudged ash on bark has become a work of art. The tree bends green and lovely still. Trammell's 72-year-old lungs are blackly creative, too, he is certain, emitting a small laugh vanishing quickly as he walks back toward the front door. Good will vanishes when he looks down these days. Fake fog at his feet, enveloping his ankles, no touch, no wetness, no white, nearly non-existent in fact but for the pieces of black swimming around inside. It makes no sound but appears to. Staring straight down at it makes it almost disappear. It is most obnoxious seen at a slant, the approximate angle of walking forward. This is the third week it has occupied Trammell's property, a foot off the ground, infecting his well-being. There in the morning, there at night, and it is obviously not in Impetus's interests to fix it. Danielle seems lovely but an idiotic bot just the same. He kicks the fake fog kicking nothing, steps through it up the driveway and sidewalk back into the house, reflexively exaggerating heel-toe as if he could walk above the fog but it is a failed attempt. The fog reorganizes immediately with each step. He shuts the door quickly to keep it outside but lets a wisp inside that drifts into a corner. He whispers "Fuck this fucking fog" and heads to the bedroom to feed Norman and get ready.

He might try Impetus again today for the sixth time to fix the leak from his neighbor Rob Cantsitstill's scrollbox. He won't get Danielle again, poor thing, probably sent back for repairs. Talk too much or get persnickety and dense and the bots just can't figure out how to respond. It's kind of fun in a vengeful analog way. It took him four months to opt out of the scroll and the headfeed and now it's going to take another four months to get Rob's leak fixed. Maybe when he gets back. When he has more time and temperament for smooth jazz on hold and the banal evil of robot kindness. Right now he has to go. He'll just barely make it as it is. The day is lost if he misses the first scroll transmission. As always, the nag of quitting murmurs deep. Whenever he is late he thinks about not going at all and just being an old man living alone with his books and with Norman and his thoughts and the forest but ends up going every time.

The morning routine: two caffeine pills, one Prilosec, two Aleve, one Zyrtec, one baby Bayer, two coughing fits, shower no shave, masturbation, two bowel movements, back-stretching tai chi routine naked on the back patio, wrapping of the penis in tissue to prevent semen and urine drippage, one bowl of sea bass and vegetable medley pate for Norman, and by 6:40 Trammell is out the door and trudging forward in his little Twigby Toyota hatchback toward City Hall. The Morning Scroll starts streaming at 7 from the Impetus transmission building in the back of City Hall and is always on time except when it crashes about once or twice or thrice a month. There is a message from last night on Trammell's landline phone that he does not see as he walks by because he despises telephones and always has it muted unless he needs a callback from someone for the newsletter. Karen answered when Trammell's brother called last summer and didn't reach him, then finally called his neighbor, the aforementioned Rob Cantsitstill, who had to walk over and tell Trammell the next day that his mother had died. One less weekly phone call for Karen to answer.

CHAPTER BOMB

Plots hatched in Hell aren't witnessed by angels.

This morning, Saturday November the 3rd, just before 7 a.m., Dick Maestro's aide, a man of little consequence beyond his usefulness as an aide, stopped working on the rewrite of a speech that had kept him up all night and that probably wouldn't be used anyway and walked into Maestro's office and told him the latest, most of which Maestro already knew:

"We believe the guy who set off the bomb was a man named Harold Dumas. As far as we know none of TRIBE's people at the top in the North Florida chapter were involved or knew it was coming. That could be a lie, covering their asses, but Dumas had no authorization that we are aware of. We'll find out. But for now we think he was a lone wolf. He may have had some help in the planning. We're checking on a Port of Jacksonville security guard who wasn't a member but was sympathetic to the cause and may have given Dumas information about schedules and unloading procedures. Dumas is listed on our books as a member, but he wasn't signed up for the port protest and he hasn't been high profile. Went to just one meeting last year. Originally from Louisiana but lives in Jacksonville now. The police and FBI don't have his name yet, as far as we know, and the four bodies inside the ship are burned beyond recognition, so they won't have confirmed IDs on them anytime soon. Probably four guys on an advance team, we're hearing, the ones who come in and unstrap the cars and prep them for unloading. Union guys. This Dumas piece of shit killed

American union guys. The ship was NYK out of Japan, so the Japanese crew would have still been on board when the bomb went off, if it had gone off somewhere else. NYK does Toyotas and Lexuses in Jacksonville before heading up to Newark. We're pretty sure Dumas set it off by remote, maybe using a drone with some kind of stealth program. I don't know how he would've gotten it attached to the hull otherwise. Security cameras all over the port. GPS monitors. Homeland guys, TSA guys everywhere. We know one of them, a supervisor, trying to reach him now, see what he knows, what they're telling him. Ship won't sink. It's not double-hulled, but the hole the bomb left wasn't that big, maybe twenty feet across, and was pretty high above the water line. The financial hit for NYK — repairs, delays in getting cars to dealers, damage to maybe three hundred cars, lawsuits from victims' families — will be pretty big but peanuts overall. We'll have to wait and see what the lasting impacts or possible positives are. More security, for sure, but could possibly impact import volume if NYK and others rethink risk. Could possibly ramp up U.S. production and new factories. Homeland and Customs and TSA and the Port Authority are all on the scene so far, along with the local police and sheriff's and bureau. FBI is the lead agency and their guys are getting ready to interview our members who were at the protest —-"

"Halt. Call Mike Wagner right now. That's the guy's name down in Jax, right? Tell him to text every member this: 'If you are asked: You do not know Harold Dumas. Delete this text immediately.' Call him now. And then text every other chapter president and tell them to get that same message out to their members. Do it in the other room. I need to call someone. Don't say a fucking word to the media yet. And tell Wagner and all the other chapter guys the same thing: Not a fucking word."

Inconsequential Man already said a fucking word to the media. He called Truth Network late last night from home, gave the editor there a heads-up on something big happening today. "Tomorrow is a new day" and "Everything changes tomorrow" was what Maestro said. Maestro thinks Inconsequential Man is a capable assistant but a limp-dicked moron otherwise. Fuck Maestro. What's on your personal phone, Maestro motherfucker? Your first mistake was trusting me to do your bidding without thinking I had a fucking spine of my own, asshole. Well you'll know soon enough I have a fucking spine. Inconsequential Man leaves the room with a hidden smile that extends from his deep groin to the corners of his small mouth.

CHAPTER NORMAN

Silence fills itself in, therefore I am.

Old deaf Norman stirs from sleep and hops down from the bed to see if the house is empty. It is, he knows once out in the hallway, padding along slowly, sleepily, because there are no smells and Trammell always has smells when he's home: smoke from his skin or a cough, cheese he's eating, moccasins that smell like dirt forest sweat. Norman is a gray and white shorthair with a Roman nose who was born to a good mother who fended off raccoons and coyotes and hid him and his siblings in the doghouse at the colony where they lived. Trammell would place a small handful of food and tin of water just outside the doghouse so she wouldn't have to walk far to eat and drink, and Norman was the first kitten to come out and let Trammell pet him, and within two months he had taken Norman and the others and their mother to be fixed. Then the rampage of white primitives living nearby began and he moved the colony deeper into the woods and brought Norman home and he was Karen's best friend for all the years until she died. The last thing she did was kiss him, Trammell holding him next to her lips. Norman understands death without understanding it. He knows it is absence that recedes over time but never ends. When Trammell goes on his daily morning trips, Norman feels doubly alone because Karen never returned that day and some small trigger remembers that. He usually sits at the sliding glass door in the family room that looks out on the backyard patio and forest. His food and water bowls are there along with a soft bed, but today Norman just goes to the glass door and sits, still groggy in the silence of deafness and absence.

The forest looks the same but isn't. Norman used to roam all around the neighborhood and knows exactly what is and isn't. Trammell is, Karen isn't, for instance. The skinny oaks he used to climb still rise up twisted to a canopy that blocks winter's cold and summer's panting sun. Beneath the canopy, branches that died look like Trammell's bony finger pointing nowhere. Trammell used to call the canopy a collaboration of self-interested leaves, back when Norman could hear. Trammell often talked to him, everyday rants and little phrases he thought were poetic or interesting in some way. He still talks to Norman, a vibration upon his deafness. Norman's eyes are starting to cloud a little too but he can still see birds he once chased and knows the different kinds Trammell has talked to him about. The big one pounding the dead branch pointing nowhere is a pileated woodpecker. Norman doesn't see many of those around anymore. They need dead branches to live and humans don't like dead branches. Never sees screech owls anymore, either. Nighttime birds that make a crying puppy sound. Norman and Trammell discovered this together once when they walked into the woods next door before so many houses were built to see if a puppy had been hit by a car or something, and then looked with the flashlight's light and saw four screech owls on a branch staring back at them, silent and small with fierce big eyes. Impossible to hunt now in such a small forest with prey depleted so the owls have moved on to dwindling elsewhere. The floods that scared Norman so when Trammell and Karen were so scared killed cedar trees and their blue berries loved by cotton mice but oaks and palmettos remain. Psycho wild grape vines still strangle the air, reaching for whatever comes next. Norman and Trammell's little patch is the last forest standing on their block. There are no vines in other yards. Norman in his wanderings used to sometimes do his business in the flower beds of neighbors but no one appreciated them as fertilizer. The Cantsitstills next door, who are always working on a noisy project of some kind to make their property as nature-free as possible, sometimes flung his bowel movements back over the fence, cursing Norman and by association Trammell as they did, landing the fresh turds with a splat on a window. Trammell left them there and watched with Norman from inside as sow bugs and palmetto bugs and little skinny creatures in the fly or wasp family ate their way through the shit until the shit was gone. Matter-of-fact miraculous, Trammell called it, the same way human bodies operate but never human minds. Norman remembers a lot about what else was out there at the other houses: stucco, grass, grass, poison, mulch, palms with blooms and berries sawed off, mulch, grass, poison, loud engine noise, gas fumes, hibiscus fragrance, tangerines on the ground under tangerine trees, lemons likewise, poison, noise, river rock that hurt to walk on, a few individual twisted oaks left standing in small groups for a windswept seaside landscape effect that essentially said fuck you to woodpeckers, owls and vines.

Until several weeks ago their backyard was huddled and safe just outside the sliding glass door. Now Norman is glad he doesn't go out anymore. Trammell says the fog along the ground doesn't hurt but it looks like it would. In any event, it can't be trusted. It looks like the flood except something in it slithers like the snakes in the marsh where Norman used to go and it has no beginning or end. It's just weird and scary and Norman doesn't like it. There is real fog today, too, drifting over land from the ocean. As scary and murky as it is, the forest somehow still makes waiting for Trammell to get back a little less lonely. It's something they've always had together, with Karen before too, a shrinking assurance as trees disappeared all around them, that cracking sound, that horrifying cracking sound of trees being killed. The fog on the ground is almost horrifying like that but with no sound. Trammell will be back soon. The day can proceed as it always does. Certainty is calming when you are old like Norman. Trammell will come in and get naked and lift weights or ride the bike thing he rides with the television on. Then he will nap for a couple of hours and Norman will join him in bed. Then in the afternoon Norman will help Trammell make calls and write and put out the newsletter in the garage by sleeping on the file cabinet next to him while he works. He will wait again while Trammell delivers the copies to the two stores that carry it free on their counters and to the one library left in the county. They will watch some TV or read at night. Then Trammell will close down the house, turn off the lights and smoke a cigarette naked on the back deck before the two of them walk back to the bedroom, where the routine is always the same and Norman loves that about it, each night the same, Trammell's smoky skin upon his fur, the breathing of words unheard into his ear.

CHAPTER SERIOUS

My family has pretty much disappeared and I am the one who made them vanish.

Children, little fucking noisemakers, squeal outside Harold Dumas' door. Ear-splitting little screams, already narcissists begging me me me. Don't bring them here, mothers. Harold is holed up with his laptop in a library study room the size of a closet in Jacksonville Beach about a mile from his home. He opened the place at 7, it is Saturday morning his regular routine, he cannot work at home. All Linda has to do is get up and appear. One sentence, one word, one sigh, one planned outing, one chore, one nag from Linda can ruin the entire enterprise before he gets started, shatter concentration with irritation, detonate passion with minutia. The library has public access wifi but he is doing nothing wrong and the reward of being able to actually get something valuable done is worth the risk. He's working on TRIBE's encrypted dark website, (the only reason he joined), so there's little chance of opposition hacks and this little room is a beautiful secret world unless fucking kids are squealing outside the closed door. Harold and Linda raised two of them but Harold detests children now. There is a time to get serious in this life and now is that time. Harold is forty-seven. His own kids grew up to be little Harolds and Lindas anyway. What he used to be before he got serious. That's really the way of the world 99 percent of the time: Mediocrity breeds mediocrity. Harold Junior is a computer sales rep just like Harold, already with a kid, and Rachel is an accountant just like her fat mom, also already with a kid and already fat. Harold has a hard time picturing the grandkids right now and doesn't want to. They are small versions with adult heads, his head and Linda's head. Kind of funny. The library should have a separate entrance for the children's section. He puts his fingers in his ears and narrows his gaze on the computer screen where his simulation drone changes color and flies through government air space undetected and scans computer files through the wall of an archive building and then seconds later blows the building up with a bomb attached to the wall. The drone leaves the scene with all interior records copied before the explosion. It is the first time the program has worked perfectly in the two years he's been working on it. He leaps inside and clenches his fist in his lap.

Suddenly the phone in his back pocket vibrates, the rush crashes, adrenaline falls, he whispers "goddammit" and retrieves his phone with a yank and reads the text, holding the phone in his lap as if it carries a disease.

"If you are asked: You do not know Harold Dumas. Delete this text immediately."

"What the fuck is this?" he whisper-screams. Harold's brain flies off the rails and at once comes the shame of being caught at something. Then another text.

"Harold, need to talk. Meet yr house, 8:30 a.m. Mike Wagner."

Harold texts back: "WTF??? K" but is not so sure that he will meet Mike Wagner at 8:30. Fear like cold methane rises, pudgy body shudders, hard plastic chair tiny sealed room terrifies.

CHAPTER SCROLL

I'm already old and just getting started.

One-Eye and the other squirrels rise up like prairie dogs on the little stone bench behind City Hall when they see the old man with the sack walking toward them. Trammell buys roasted peanuts in the shell at the farmer's market and keeps them in his car. The squirrels chatter hello give us our nuts and Trammell says hello just hold your horses, little ones. They hang out near the Impetus transmission building solely because of Trammell's daily nuts, huddling in a little patch of palmettos and mangroves at the edge of the marsh next to the maintenance building. Later in the day they return to the scattered oaks in the yards nearby where they nest and sleep and live and eat bird seed. Trammell sits down and puts peanuts on the bench and on the gravel below the bench and saves a couple to hand personally to One-Eye, who lost it to a hawk's talon or a fight with another male or maybe just ran into a palmetto frond's tip, which can cut corneas. In any event, the left eye is sightless white now and One-Eye tilts his head toward his vision and gently grabs Trammell's two fingers with his scrawny little claws and sits back to crack open the shell. He and the other squirrels say thank you in their way. It is warm as always in November but the ocean is warmer, and real fog smelling lightly of salt and seaweed settles around Trammell and the squirrels and becomes a murky, loving containment. Real fog is welcome to him, so much more lifelike. This is the journalism he does now, and despite his daily reluctance he usually embraces it once he arrives at the bench each day. It already feels old and reliable, a sliver of something useful and proper. The world slows down sitting here each morning as it simultaneously accelerates everywhere else.

A flying V of pelicans, seventeen of them, glides through the fog toward the marsh avoiding power lines. Florida still occasionally exists.

Looking at them in groggy peace, Trammell's heart jumps when The Morning Scroll snaps to life — little optic fiber firecrackers going off as usual at 7 o'clock sharp. His heart calms and he settles in on the bench with his notepad and pen as One-Eye and his mates Doctor DoLittle all around him.

"Hello, Flagler Beach neighbor. Welcome to your personalized news feed, The Morning Scroll," says the woman's voice, lying from the get-go, nothing personalized about the general feed that leaves the operations center first, essentially just an advertisement that can be seen from the street before dispersing into the personalized scrolls that subscribers get, wrapped around their house every morning like a moving translucent ribbon, not a real woman's voice either, a blended assertive calm from a voice logarithm similar to the airport's but more seductive. Impetus wants to give its male subscribers a slight hard-on and its female subscribers a slight swoon. Trammell has a source — not a friend, he makes a point to have no friends beyond cats and squirrels and writers of books — who works at Impetus in IT who told him the marketing guys instructed his team to make the voice "luxuriantly female." The male voice was supposed to be "commanding and compassionate."

"Here are today's headlines," says Luxuriant Female. The true and false and partial and malicious begin to flow onto the screen. Trammell only fact-checks local news about his city, Flagler Beach, which scrolls first followed by county news, state, national, politics, sports, entertainment and business. The entire aggregate flows out of the transmission building before customizing at each subscriber's scrollbox, so by coming here Trammell is able to keep an especially close eye on news generated or picked up by two local websites — willynilly.com and ironheel.com — that routinely send out lies, the former from mostly carelessness and the latter from a deep misunderstanding of patriotism. A twentysomething surfer named Mike Jaynes runs willynilly, and mostly just wants to keep the site rockin' with comments and tweets and guest articles about what to eat and where to hang out, but he has a little news section too with posts from other sites and a popup every minute or so called 'Overheard at Tierra Tavern.' A quick look at City Hall records and a couple of phone calls usually counters willynilly quickly and makes for an easy day. Ironheel is more problematic. The man who runs it is retired Army and a local official in TRIBE who has the advertising support of the NRA, Americans for Prosperity and Return to Greatness. He is listed in state records as Frederick Branch, registered agent for the nonprofit ironheel.com, but his online moniker is The Colonel, and his website has quickly gained a national following after starting as a small-time regional site. Old farts like The Colonel who find their cause late in life are dangerous folk, emboldened by and embraced for unyielding perspective. Trammell has never met The Colonel but knows the type. Uber Patriot old white guys. A couple of parttime staffers at ironheel actually sometimes talk to sources and look at records for local stories, but the local element has shrunk to a hard-to-find link on the home page as the site gained traction nationally by breaking "stories" from the TRIBE playlist. TRIBE supplies the stories through a direct feed that posts them after The Colonel rubber-stamps them and uploads. Trammell has no desire or ability to debunk TRIBE's national reports and just focuses on the misleading local items. They move on the scroll more prominently than the website, and the one that moves first today is typical: a story on the mayor's personal dock on the canal behind his house. It takes nine or ten seconds to move across the transmission building's outdoor screen and the prominence of all-caps tells Trammell it's ironheel crap and destined for customized TRIBE subscribers. Trammell reads it while scribbling notes:

Mayor Beechum used tax dollars to rebuild dock

That new dock behind Mayor Allen Beechum's house was paid for by you and me to the tune of nearly $12,000. The MAYOR GOT A FREE RIDE by latching onto a federal grant that covered canal dredging and public dock rebuilding. THE MONEY WAS NOT MEANT TO BE USED ON THE PRIVATE DOCKS OF ELECTED OFFICIALS. Beechum denied any wrongdoing, but records show that the dock at his address was included in the rebuilding plan, at a cost of $11,765. ironheel.com

Trammell knows what the young reporter at ironheel does not know or did not choose to report under The Colonel's direction. Beechum is a retired lit professor who wants to expand parks and beach access and beautify downtown and generally spend tax money in ways that irritate The Colonel and his flock. Trammell wrote a short op-ed about the dock issue in The Daily Truth a week ago. The mayor did indeed latch onto the federal grant, but he repaid the money to the city. It was a strange, ripe-for-abuse public/private grant program that allowed private citizens to 'opt-in' on the dredging/rebuilding project if they paid their portion of the cost. Five others along with the mayor did it because it came out cheaper for them than hiring someone on their own. Trammell wrote that Beechum should have made the financial arrangement clear from the start and probably not have touched it to begin with. The Colonel's youngster obviously didn't read the entire grant proposal and budget details or care to reprint Beechum's full comments. The simple, necessary stuff of reporting. He and The Colonel also clearly hadn't seen Trammell's opinion piece, and that's not surprising. The Daily Truth has a circulation of about 250. Jaynes reads it at willynillly, Trammell knows because they've talked about it, but he and The Colonel have never met.

The Beechum item should be easy to write after he checks ironheel's full story to make sure they didn't by some slim chance get it right farther down in the copy. Trammell is always looking for an easy day so he can interact with as few humans as possible and nap in the late morning before writing the newsletter. The only other item that needs addressing is the third one that scrolled about the city's plans to add more seawall along the dunes that washed away in the last hurricane for the 10th time. The city isn't extending its seawall, as willynilly wrongly reported based on a beach activist's tweet, but simply bringing in more huge granite boulders to stabilize A1A that is a foot or so away from dropping into the sea. It's already been rebuilt twice. That one should be fairly easy, too. The can gets kicked farther down the beach by officials and the city prepares to fall into the sea.

One-Eye and the other squirrels have moved on and Trammell closes his notepad and lifts his old bones from the bench to leave when Luxuriant Female breaks into the scroll with an announcement of National Breaking News. Impetus sends the alerts across its national network, so the voice activation kicks in and overrides the normal silent feed. Trammell hates it when it blares from his neighbors' scrolls, but here it's only a little jarring and he stands still to listen.

"At least four workers are dead after an explosion blew a hole in the hull of a cargo ship carrying Toyota SUVs as it docked in the Port of Jacksonville this morning. Federal and state investigators have not released details other than to say they are looking into the possibility of a terrorist attack. The explosion occurred at about 6 a.m. as members of TRIBE staged a rally protesting the import of foreign cars into an American port. Through its national president Dick Maestro, TRIBE released a statement saying that it in no way promotes or tolerates violence and had nothing to do with today's tragic event. Maestro said the organization immediately began an investigation into any possible involvement by rogue "lone wolves" and has credible evidence that the bomber was a plant from the opposition, possibly the Democratic National Committee, attempting to sabotage the rally and link TRIBE candidate Daniel Hammerschmidt with this senseless violence three days before Tuesday's election. The statement went on to say that TRIBE is seeking a full investigation into President Holland's possible role in the murder of four Americans. The White House issued a statement that did not address TRIBE's accusations directly except to strongly deny them. In a separate statement President Holland said: 'Our hearts and prayers go out to the families of the victims in this horrific act. I promise those families and the American people that I will commit the full resources of the FBI and Homeland Security and the City of Jacksonville to investigate this bombing and capture the criminals who carried it out as quickly as possible. At this time we do not believe there is a continuing threat of additional violence, and our first priority now and always is the safety of the American people.' This is a developing story. Check your scroll, television, thoughtext or headfeed for updates. And be sure to go to MyImpetus.com for details on MyScroll Discount Days continuing all through November."

Trammell sits back down on the bench in the stillness of Luxuriant Female's voice ending and news and marketing fall like ash to the earth around him.

CHAPTER PULITZER

Remember the Maine! To hell with Spain!

Alright, students, we'll get things started today with what most scholars call the first press-driven war. We must put it in the proper context of course, about 100,000 years of context: From the moment humans began communicating with one another, truth has been manipulated and massaged. A prehistoric hunter tells a rival about the mammoth that got away, and the legend grows with each telling. A 16th century Italian court sends a newsletter, called an avisso, into the public square, stirring up dissent with propaganda about a rival. A Town Crier spins the king's news in England centuries ago. A press secretary flatters the president last week. History shows that truth has never existed unvarnished in the public domain, but is instead a cultural narrative constantly shifting, curving, collapsing and being reborn as something different and new. And when truth changes, history responds. Today I'm going to tell you about two New York newspapers that battled for profits and power and ended up shaping public opinion to the point where the United States went to war with Spain over Cuba. Dictators and other authoritarian governments, of course, have always controlled the media to shape truth in their favor, but in this case a free press did most of the shaping. If you could hold your questions until the end—

Yes, Rob from Flagler Beach. You have a question before I can complete the sentence asking you to hold your questions.

Sorry, Professor Ibid, but why is your belief that truth has never existed any more valid than my belief that truth does exist. For instance, I'm eating ham and eggs right now that are mighty tasty, and that's true without a doubt.

The pig and several Jews and Muslims I know would probably disagree with you, Rob, but you make a good point. Personal truths — this ham is delicious — are very different from the broader truths that propel a society or nation — We must fight this or that evil. And the first often leads to the second. Adolph Hitler, for example, was a so-so young artist living in poverty in Vienna, mingling with Jewish patrons and dealers in the art community. But he was a nut with a deluded ego who came under the spell of Viennese racists. He developed visions of an ever grander Aryan opera under his control, and hatred of Jews became the unifying force in service to his artistic vision. We all know where that ended up. His personal truth — Jews are vermin to be exterminated — was adopted by – or more accurately, ignited – in millions of Germans and became his nation's cultural truth. Insanity on a national scale can be truth. Evil can be truth. And of course, Hitler's truth has staying power even today in several of our most recent presidential candidates and their followers. So thanks for raising the point, Rob from Flagler Beach, but if others could hold their questions until the end of each workshop section it would be appreciated.

So, how is this 100,000 year old ever-changing truth created? One way is discovery. Think of physics. The physical sciences. We look at a tree's wood and can say with complete confidence that this bark, this wood is hard. Knock it with your knuckles and there's all the proof you need, right? Well, no. Hard to the touch, yes, but scientific discovery over centuries makes that truth less true. It is spongy cellulose, water coursing through vessels, cells, chemicals, molecules, atoms, neutrons, protons, electrons, quarks, and parasites, mold, fungi, methane and dust. So rather than a piece of wood only being hard, it is many things, and many truths.

Another catalyst for creating new truth — and this one propels most of the broader cultural truths that shape history — is motive. A fascist government, for instance, wants citizens to overlook their problems and unite in fear of an embellished or invented common enemy. A minister of propaganda or even a president will manipulate the messages that citizens receive to accomplish this goal, using what used to be called disinformation or propaganda but is often known today as 'alternative facts.' The motive is not always nefarious. In the legend of Cerberus mentioned earlier, ancient storytellers and poets wanted their version to be the most daring and exciting, so they exaggerated or altered truth with each telling. No harm, no foul. But our two New York newspapers essentially did the same thing as they battled for readers and influence, and a seemingly innocent push for profits ended up costing American lives. The most daring and exciting headlines win, and there is no more daring and exciting headline than the big bold letters WAR!

The newspapers were led by two giants of journalism in the late 19th and early 20th centuries. William Randolph Hearst was publisher of the New York Journal, and Joseph Pulitzer, for whom journalism's highest honor is named, published the New York World. Their rivalry was fierce, even down to the comics. Pulitzer had a comic with a yellow-dressed character called The Yellow Kid, and Hearst hired away the artist. Then Pulitzer came back with another yellow kid character. And thus was born the term yellow journalism, meaning an overly dramatic style that exaggerates truth. Otherwise known as sensationalism.

This approach to the truth helped start the Spanish-American War. Hearst was the main instigator here, and he had personal ambition as a motive along with profit. You may be familiar with the movie "Citizen Kane," in which the director and star Orson Welles used Hearst as a model for the title character.

Yes, Rob from Flagler Beach.

Orson who? and Citizen who?

Welles and Kane. Just a side note, really. Won't be on the test.

Thanks, professor.

Back to our lesson. To beat Pulitzer at his own game, Hearst sent his best reporters down to Cuba to report on the worst of Spanish colonialism and oppression: stories on female prisoners, executions, valiant rebels fighting and starving women and children. But the biggest story to come out of the war wasn't even true. After the sinking of the Maine, the Hearst newspapers, with no evidence, unequivocally blamed the Spanish, and soon U.S. public opinion demanded intervention. Turns out the Spanish didn't do it. There was an explosion inside the Maine. It blew itself up. But that sensational headline and story, more than any other, sparked the war that the U.S. won in about twelve weeks, establishing itself as a world power with an empire of its own in the Philippines, Puerto Rico, Cuba (for a while) and Guam, all gained from the Spanish. The war also made Hearst one of the most powerful men in the country. All the politicians and the money men knew now that a free press, not just a state-controlled press, was capable of starting a war.

CHAPTER TIP

One of your best sources is the smallest detail.

Trammell's plummet after the bombing news report lasted fifteen minutes as the fog settled around him, slowly brightened by a higher sun. One-Eye and the other squirrels scampered back thinking there might be more nuts but the old man just sat there on the bench staring at the ground with his reporter's notebook fallen from his hand. Then One-Eye stepped onto his shoe and made him laugh, breaking the plummet's spell, and Trammell stood slowly and left. Now he drives home from City Hall in an ease of absurdity. The violence of the bombing and the lies in the reporting have blown like sand against a wall. Nothing an old man can do about it. The Prophets of The Dumb will prevail, a lifetime has shown.

Trammell arrives home, rolling the car through the real fog hugging the street and over the fake fog leaking out onto the driveway under his old good friends the trees. Notebook tucked under his arm, he turns his sidewalk's corner through the forest stepping through the fake fog and sees Rob Cantsitstill standing akimbo at the front door, wearing his trademark coaching shorts with white socks and work boots. Rob is a tall thin retired electrician, built like bundled wire on bone. Trammell startles him and he turns and shudders and then looks awkwardly ashamed before puffing out his chest again.

"You scared the shit out of me! I thought you were inside."

"Nope, just back from city hall. Didn't you see my car was gone? What's up?"

"You've got to start turning on your phone, Trammell. Luckily this time it wasn't about your mother. Some guy from Truth Network left you a message last night on your phone and then called me this morning when you didn't call him back. Didn't say what it was about but said it was urgent. Here's his name and number."

Rob holds his phone up for Trammell to see, and Trammell lifts his eyes and puts on his reading glasses. He writes down the name – James Dunbar, a stunning little surprise, his best reporter long ago at the Picayune – and the number, a 202 in Washington. Then Trammell sees in a split-second glance the all-caps TRIBE in the list of text messages and pretends he needs to double check the phone number to get Rob to hold the phone up longer.

"If you are asked: You do not know Harold Dumas. Delet ..." the partial text reads.

Trammell asks, "Aren't you a member of TRIBE, Rob? Were you at the rally this morning when the bomb went off?"

"I didn't go. I'm taking an online workshop this morning and have to get back to it. We're on a break now. Then Rhonda's got me doing another project this afternoon. Pressure washing the house again. You know she likes it spotless. Wanted to go to the rally but couldn't. Pretty shitty what happened. Somebody trying to make it look like it was us. It was a plant, though, from our rich bitch president and the Democrats to screw with the election."

"That's what TRIBE says, anyway. Think that's the truth?"

"Nothing those snowflakes do would surprise me. Oh, sorry.

Forgot you were one of them."

Trammell laughs and half-twirls like a ballerina. He is fairly certain that Rob wonders if he was one of those married gays who's coming out in old age now that Karen is gone. Trammell no longer argues social, personal, cultural or political points with people like Rob. He bids him thanks and goodbye with a smile. The name Harold Dumas tickles his memory as he walks inside and closes the door. A fluff of fake fog slips inside. Rob, somehow, did not notice it even though he is its cause.

CHAPTER LOVERS

It takes courage to not be discouraged.

"Harold never said anything."

"About what?"

"About me losing weight. He never once said anything."

"I did. A lot. I knew you were trying hard."

"I know you did. That's why I love you. But I still feel terrible about Harold. We raised a family together, built a life such as it was. I knew he hated being around me anymore but he also trusted me."

"Don't beat yourself up, baby. The only thing Harold loved was his research, thought he could save the world from terrorism with his little stealth drones. He took you for granted. Now it's coming back to bite him. He'll be put away for the rest of his little drone life. Or he'll be on the run until he can't run anymore. Either way. His choice."

"But he didn't do it."

"How many times do we have to go through this, baby? It does not matter what someone does or doesn't do in this world. What matters most is what people believe about you. I am a plumber, but I have created someone who is much more than a plumber. You have done the same. The whole axis tilts toward perception and the enhancement of truth, and you have to understand that if you want to accomplish anything valuable. Every great cause is an enhancement of truth."

"You talk a good game, Mike. But all Harold wanted to do

was something valuable. Something worthwhile. He thought it could save American lives if a drone could infiltrate computers through a wall. When he first started we were kind of in it together. Then he just drifted farther and farther away."

"I understand that, Linda, but all of this we're doing is for the greater good. What's going to happen to Harold is for the greater good. All that we've been through the last year is for the greater good. And for our greater good, too, you and me."

Linda Dumas sat in the passenger seat of the black Lincoln Navigator parked in her own driveway. Mike Wagner sat behind the wheel with the car still running and the tinted windows rolled up. It was 8:25 on Saturday morning. Harold was supposed to meet Mike at 8:30 and Mike isn't sure if he's home yet. His car could be in the garage.

"I guess you're right, but I still don't know, I'm still not sure of any of this. It's so hard I feel like I'm going to throw up."

"Nothing worthwhile is easy, baby. But it will mean you and me can be together and all the work we've done in the last year to get Harold's research into the right hands and getting the right man into the White House will be worth it. We're the only ones in Jacksonville who know, and we need to be the ones who are with Harold when he gets arrested. My guy in Washington said the police are coming at eight thirty-five, so let's go inside, see if Harold's there yet, and talk to him and try to calm him down before they get here. He's going to be wondering why we're together, and let's just give it to him straight. But even more he's going to wonder what the hell is going on with that text. Remember what we say: We don't know why everyone got that text, and we're here to try and figure out why. Then the cops come in."

"Okay. Give me a minute. I need a minute. I'm letting my husband know about us and that he might be a suspect in this bombing and I helped you because I thought it was for the greater good, but I am not brave and I am not evil, and you're asking me to be both. Give me a fucking minute, Mike."

CHAPTER FUGITIVE

Hiding is what humans do.

Something is happening beyond the sky, dominion over minds and events by some larger force unknown unseen. Harold's immediate world of house and job and research and Linda is a sick panic and at the same time someone or something like gods on Olympus or a secret cabal of the ultrapowerful is out to kill him or harm him in some way he cannot imagine or even grasp as a concept except for an image of his fingernails being pulled back and his throat being slashed. The drone software is just research, for heaven's sake. Are they making some connection with the port bombing? Should have never joined TRIBE, bunch of blue-collar primitives. Harold has never been cool or in the cool crowd but he has never been hated or hunted, either. Fucking TRIBE caused it all. Every sensation wired. He has no plan except hiding. He rushed out of the library with his laptop under his arm and drove home without speeding and parked down the street from where he lives and walked trying to appear normal to the house across the street and now squats behind the hibiscus hedge of his neighbors' yard, watching his house in trembling impotent anger masking deep marrow fear.

Harold tries to think. He doesn't even know Wagner. He's only met him once, at the lone meeting he went to last year so his membership would kick in, and he struck Harold as arrogant and dismissive, a plumbing contractor newly addicted to power. He doesn't trust him at all. And he was making eyes at Linda, of all things, too. Must be one of those guys who likes fat women. Why the fuck should he meet someone he doesn't trust or know at all after that weird text? Harold only joined TRIBE because he wanted access to the members website and its dark web links, not to get fucked over or killed by some punk plumber. The coral hibiscus bloom tickles his nose and he yanks the bloom off with a wrapped fist. Why are Roger's and Lisa's hibiscus blooming and not his? They live in Maine and don't touch them nine months out of the year and he babies his to fucking death. Harold takes deep breaths to refocus his attention and fear.

At 8:25 a black Lincoln Navigator pulls into Harold's driveway and no one gets out for five minutes or more behind tinted windows with the car running. Harold can't hear the engine from across the street but sees the wavy heat of the exhaust. Some of it blows on his hibiscus beside the driveway. Finally a man who looks like Wagner with the fu manchu but heavier, must have gained weight in a year, gets out of the car. And a woman, big, wait, Linda, LINDA, gets out of the passenger side. Linda Linda Linda what are you doing Linda and they walk to the front door and Wagner rings the doorbell while Linda stands behind him with her head down. Wagner scratches his balls and repositions his package while he waits. Linda turns away from the door and looks like she's crying. Harold thinks she may have lost weight, seen from this distance. No one is home, maybe they'll just leave, but then the door opens and a tall skinny man Harold does not know with wispy long hair stands in shadow in the doorway and reaches out his hand as if to shake Wagner's but raises a gun instead and fires two shots in Wagner's chest and stomach and Wagner falls back from the force and whacks his head on the concrete sidewalk and stays down without moving and blood begins to trickle onto the white sidewalk and Linda screams and turns to run but she's still big and Harold sees the thump in the back and shoulder blade and the lurch forward into the hibiscus by the door like easy violence in a movie and the longhaired man tosses the gun down on the welcome mat in front of Wagner's body and Harold recognized the sound and now the shape as it lies there. It is his gun that killed Wagner and Linda.

Harold stares at the crumpled hibiscus beneath Linda. Is she still alive? He cannot help her. She's moving, lifting her arm. He cannot help her. He must, he cannot. Helpless. Neighbors are already peering out windows and looking out cracked doors. Someone has surely called 911. He cannot, can he? Does he want to? Then sirens arrive, how so fucking fast? Something that feels like a giant hand lifts Harold and moves him somehow and he crawls through the shrubs to the back of Roger's and Lisa's house and runs to the next street over and reaches his car panting and cranks it and leaves at a normal speed before any perimeter is set up, going he knows not where. I had no options, Linda.

CHAPTER RESURRECTION

Could you please take me off the dumbshit beat?

Trammell walks into the family room and eases around Norman asleep on the wood floor so that he doesn't scare him. Trammell puts his hand on the floor in front of Norman's nose and Norman smells him and jumps a little then meows loudly hello. He can't hear himself meow, so the volume varies wildly.

"Hello to you, young man." Trammell scoops him up and kisses his head. "It's a pretty good time to be deaf, Norman. Nothing but noise out there. You should be thankful."

You smell like smoke, Norman says, and Trammell agrees. "I know. You and Karen always hate the smoke. It's coming out of my pores. But you'll just have to live with it. I'm not quitting until I'm dead." He puts Norman down and Norman stands there for a second or two getting his bearings.

"I've got to call someone I used to know, really a world I used to know, it's been so long. That's the world that ended up destroying my brain, as I've discussed with you many times."

Yes, you have, ad nauseum in fact, Norman says, wandering over to his food dish, glad to have Trammell back home.

In the kitchen Trammell checks Truth Network's coverage on his computer, reads through the lead story and then picks up the land line to call.

"Hello, Trammell."

"God, I hate caller ID. I'm all ready to say Hi, James this is Trammell returning your call but then I have to stop and rethink my first sentence."

"(laughs) Trammell, you're as perky and chipper as ever. And if you haven't quite mastered caller ID, are you at least taking advantage of that newfangled device called a TV?"

"Sometimes. Except all of the nature shows are reruns. James, I've got a name for you to check out in the TRIBE bombing: Harold Dumas."

"And how the hell are *you*, Trammell? I haven't talked to you in, what, ten years and you're already working the day's top story. How did you know that's why I called."

"I assumed. Why else? I'm not exactly your cherished mentor-slash-father figure. I read ya'll's stuff just now, one of the few reasons I go online, and you're kicking ass pretty good after TRIBE sent out the first batch of lies. Does that name sound familiar to you at all? Did a Dumas work at the Picayune?"

"It doesn't ring any bell. Where'd you get it? I've got a source in Dick Maestro's office up here, one of his aides, that tipped me last night to something big happening this morning involving TRIBE, but he didn't know the details. Now I guess he does. I can't call him back because he says his phone isn't secure. He'll have to call me. Where'd you get this Harold Dumas?"

"Pure serendipity, as you know a journalist's best friend. My neighbor, the one you called to reach me, he's a member of TRIBE. Saw an odd text message on his phone when I was getting your name and number off of it. The text said 'You do not know Harold Dumas.' Then I think it said delete the message, but that part was cut off.

Why would they send that message to my goof neighbor only an hour or so after the bombing?"

"Has to mean something. I'm running it through Googly now."

"So will everyone else once it gets out. Does anyone else have it?"

"Haven't heard it until you."

A short stretch of silence during which Trammell thinks back. "Remember when you asked me to get you off the social services beat? I always remember that it was so funny. You called it 'dumbshit fatigue.' That's what I have now."

"Yes, I remember. An elitist in training. Here's something very strange. Harold Dumas barely exists, apparently. He has no digital footprint to speak of. The only thing that comes up in a search are a few other Harold Dumases in obits, and for the one who might be our guy with a Jacksonville Beach address I just see a members list in the ACLU, a petition he signed for Earth Liberation Front, a couple of Faceface mentions on the Democratic National Committee page of all things, a President Holland PAC supporter and a few pay sites like PeopleFinders. No LinkedEnd, no Faceface or Twitwit, no mention of anything related to the Picayune. Doesn't sound much like a TRIBE guy."

"I'll bet most of those sites are fake. Somebody set up a fake profile. Changed his history. Seriously, the Earth Liberation Front? That's the dead giveaway. Some Russian hacker wouldn't have known they haven't been around in any significant way for years.

Maybe I'm a lefty conspiracy theorist, but it seems like he's being set up as the plant."

"Wise old sage becomes wacky old nut. It does make sense, though."

"And I know where I know Dumas from. It was an article after Katrina. Something we did after Katrina. The Superdome coverage, maybe. Do you still have access to the full library?"

"I don't know if my code still works. I'll try."

"I'd help but I don't want to turn my computer back on."

"Fine, Trammell. Read the papyrus while I look." Fifteen seconds of silence. "Yes, holy shit, the code still works. And here it is. You were right, Trammell. Sheri wrote it. Remember Sheri? Tall redhead, really good writer, really nice legs, incredible calves. Anyway, Dumas was an IT manager at the Superdome, talking about how they converted most of their system for the recovery operation. Actually a pretty cool story. They had to do it on their own, because FEMA was so disorganized and late. I remember it now."

"Didn't Sheri always save her notebooks?"

"Against the advice of the attorneys, yes. Dated them and archived them. Notebooks and discs. A little OCD going on with her, but it's one reason she was so good."

"Maybe she can track down a cell phone number for Dumas. A long shot, but you never know."

"It'd be a miracle if A) Sheri has notes from that long ago, and B) Dumas still has the same phone."

"Unless he's an old school geek."

"Doubt it. He's IT. But maybe he's hanging onto some cherished flip-top or just kept transferring the same number to new phones. Worth a shot. I'll try to reach Sheri and see if she has anything, but in the meantime, I need your help on this story, Trammell, to be sort of a tutor. That's the real reason I called."

"I don't do journalism anymore, James, except for a little daily newsletter here in town. I also have given up completely on the human species. So I wouldn't be a good influence on any young bright minds."

"I just need you to be wise and experienced, Trammell, not a savior. We've hired a young investigative reporter who just got laid off from the Times-Union and she seems to be very good but I just need someone who can give her a steady hand. We've already got our main guy in Jax at the scene right now, so you and her will need to pursue other angles. I'd start with finding out as much as you can about Dumas. Can you meet with her today?"

"I really can't, James. Maybe after I get my workout and my nap and my newsletter out. And like I said, I really don't do journalism anymore. Brain's pretty much gone. Death by digital."

"Doesn't matter. I know you too well. You always said you weren't worth a shit and then you were always worth many shits. My stories were always better after you. Always. So I'm calling her and telling her to meet you at the Starbucks in St. Augustine Beach at 9. Halfway between you and her. She's in south Jacksonville. And then I need one more big thing from you, Trammell. I need you to dredge up your old skills from the misanthrope dungeon and interview the guy who runs ironheel.com. He lives in Flagler Beach. Can you do it?"

"No, I can't. Shit, man, you're getting me deeper into this than I want to be. But I will as a favor to you, James, because I didn't have to rewrite every story you wrote. Can't tell you what that meant to my sanity and my soul. Mediocrity just fucking wears you out over time. You were one of the ones who staved that off a little. But I hate coffee and I hate Starbucks. Too many digital zombies in one place."

"Thanks for whatever it is you just said. The ironheel guy goes by The Colonel –

"I know him. Of him, anyway. Never met him. Just correct his website's lies every day."

"In what, a newsletter? It has to be something print."

"You got it. Borrowed from your name. The Daily Truth. Just local news. Kind of a fact check service. Borrowed the font from the Picayune."

"Send me a copy sometime. Anyway, the reporter's name is Lucy Neale, she's a light-skinned black woman in her mid-twenties who looks even younger than that. She has lots of freckles. She'll be looking for you, too. I'll tell her to look for an old white guy who never smiles. Do you still have a beard?"

"Yes. Unruly Civil War goatee."

"Trammell's last stand. Thanks for doing this. Do you wear the weird beard so people will leave you alone?"

"Well, yes, partly. But mostly because Karen's not around so

I don't have a woman nagging me about how much nicer a trimmed beard looks."

Starts to laugh, doesn't. "I didn't know, Trammell. I'm sorry."

"No worries, James. It's distant and intimate. I'll help your reporter any way I can."

CHAPTER HEAVEN

After inhaling the crushed leaves of the Angel's trumpet, she alternated between murmuring incomprehensibly and uttering loud, heart-rending shrieks, and her limbs became hideously contorted before her last breath silenced all external signs of life quite suddenly.

Donnie Bone needed stuff real real real bad more than 24 hours now and he had killed two people for God's sake but he held off, he held off for Baby so she could try it first and get the first buzz. Now that's fucking Love. Donnie drove gripping the wheel with one hand and sitting on the other to stop it from shaking and dripping forehead sweat melting inside and head bursting but it was more than just needing stuff. It was crazier than that like a wild empty hole with thoughts not lining up right because of the fat woman he killed. He keeps feeling mentally sick about the fat woman because she didn't just look scared as shit and shocked as shit like the dude but she also looked kinda sad, too, like she knew it was coming and was so helpless about where to go and what to do and so fucking kind, so kind in her scared scared eyes, made him feel like a monster. But he didn't really have a fucking choice. He's got no fucking money and he's got no stuff for him and Baby. This was a turnaround move, man, turn things around and maybe get a foot in the door to something else. He'd've been a fool not to and he didn't really have a choice, lady. He's sorry but it was, like, he had to.

The Corolla's brakes squeal like the bandsaw at work used to when he worked and Donnie pulls over with black exhaust pouring out in the right lane blocking traffic, leans over and yells out the passenger side window at Baby, selling tomatoes they get from her dad at a stand that Donnie built one weekend. He always and still knows how to build things.

"Close it down and come'on, Baby, we gotta go, now."

Baby's got a son in foster care who's six now she thinks and she was missing him in the deeply despairing way she gets when she imagines the neverland of being a real mother when Donnie drove up and shouted. She wakes up from the mother dream and gets shaken and mad about the interruption and shouts back to the car, "What the fuck are you talkin' about, Donnie?"

"Never mind, Baby, I just got somethin' you're gonna like. Now close it down and get in."

Baby jumps and claps and whoops — just everything, everything, fucking changed in one second — and closes down the stand in seconds slamming plywood over the tomatoes and races to the car, her boobies bouncing. She still has those and Donnie still appreciates them although the rest of her looks like shit.

"Where'd you get it? I been sick all morning. I almost threw up on a fucking customer," Baby says once she's inside the car and they're taking off, almost running into a Lincoln pickup going by, "and where'd you get the money?"

"I got a job. I got hired for a job. And it might lead to other jobs. They're only paying me in stuff this time, but it's supposed to be really good shit, like, mind-blowing shit. We might be able to sell some of it, like to Jim or that Bradley guy you give blow jobs to for stuff. I just picked it up and got a little taste ready for you. Look in the glove."

Baby hurries her hand to the glove and reaches for the little packet of crushed up pills.

"Pretty big chunks, aren't they?" She dips her pinky fingernail into the bag.

"I didn't have my pounder. Stop complainin'. Take a coupla hits and let me know." They both laugh.

"What kind of job?" Baby leans and sniffs deep and wipes her nose, licks her finger. "Oh, shit, Donnie. This shit is heaven."

Donnie reaches for the bag and the little spoon in the ashtray and dips it in the bag while he's driving and has it right up underneath his nose when Baby starts humming real low like a gurgle staring straight ahead and he screams What's wrong, Baby and pulls off the road onto the dirt shoulder and she starts shaking and jerking her arms and shoulders and sweating all over her face with her neck veins popping out and coughing and shrieking, just fucking shrieking, and then spewing blood splattering on the dash and while she does her scared wide blood-red eyes look over at Donnie and she spasms again and again and Donnie doesn't know what to say at first but then starts screaming at her like it's her fault and trying to think where the hospital is and then shouts "Baby, no!" and shouts almost as loud "I killed Baby! These bastards tried to kill me and they killed Baby!" and Donnie was right about Baby. She gurgled and choked and then stopped moving and slumped forward in the seat and all the air left her and her back stopped moving in and out and her blond hair on her blue shirt stopped moving, no breaths no nothing, from alive to dead, dead Baby dead dead Baby Baby dead and not waking up. Donnie shook her and shouted some more and the world inside the car collapsed, the world smothered him, the center of his body twisted and heaving and it seems like only a second ago Baby had just been saying "This is heaven."

Donnie shaking like strung out but weaker and different like coils inside but he gets his muscles to work and leans her back up slowly so as not to hurt her not to hurt Baby. He's shaking with no leg strength and he's a total fucking freakout, and tries to make her look like she's sleeping, leans over and kisses her cheek and weeps into her, tries to shake his head back into real time and turns the Corolla around and decides right there to drive south toward Flagler Beach, where the motherfucking Colonel supposedly lives.

CHAPTER IMPRECISE

Beautiful science/purple orange blue unfolds/above the dark west.

The Colonel does not let his fury show even in a massive house alone. His response to error, to imprecision, as always, is hard-nosed efficiency, the crew-cut emotion of the military. The ocean laps quietly with waves like a lake and a light rain falls with no wind. Cotton fog crawls inland over the dunes and onto his patio presenting on the windows as dripping mist. A lack of wind lives permanently inside. The Colonel's huge house holds vacant air, a home without a wife, decorated by her, left unchanged and cared for, dusted, vacuumed, straightened by the solitary soldier. It felt odd to do domestic chores at first but as days passed continuing to do them became necessary and true. All of the furniture, paint, tile, paintings, walls, mirrors are Li. The Colonel heads to his office in the garage and slows to look at pillows she bought with him saying yes they're pretty just to get out of the store. Her art and her toughness held together there by floral fabric. They are square cloth scenes from an English garden, blooms interrupted by the edges, "tranquil and disruptive at the same time, don't you think, Colonel?" She had precision in her lack of precision. The Colonel's anger is leavened by her as he walks through the foyer, the dining room, the huge house, her niches of color and wildness, never too wild, what his life needed. He nears the garage and shakes off thoughts of Li that are sliding toward loneliness. There is a task, a problem, a mission. Longing and vacancy narrow to purpose. The Colonel is a fit man of seventy and his mind mirrors his body: religiously precise, with an ability to compartmentalize that served him well in his years in cyber command, the Army's multifarious division, no threat ever retreating, new threats always advancing. Entering his garage, a memory of Li helping him set up the office tries to conjure sadness but is fought back. He refocuses on facts. Li saw only the first two editions before she died, back when he only updated the website once a week and reached a few hundred subscribers. The ironheel universe is now ten thousand times that, a prospect The Colonel never imagined nor desired but now embraces. The TRIBE fee and partnership as their primary news feed propelled him from the small base of retired military guys in Flagler Beach to a national audience of TRIBE members. He was apprehensive at first when TRIBE's president Dick Maestro called but soon welcomed the challenge with Li gone. The Colonel expanded his software and hardware and the garage headquarters setup to handle the growth. A huge screen with the ironheel homepage dominates the wall next to the house, surrounded by aggregate sites and feeds on smaller screens. Li never saw any of this. She would not approve. She saw it coming. More hardliners involved, you growing more hardline, more rigid, less kind. Alright, Li, that's enough. Focus. Everything is working fine except for the huge screen, which stares down unmoving and locked.

At his oak desk, The Colonel curses the hack, curses how he let it through, curses why the safeguards failed, gets all of the self-pity out of the way so he can concentrate. The problem, obvious: The TRIBE feed on the bombing posted itself, without his approval or upload, and positioned its play on the homepage as the lead item fixed on the page. The Colonel cannot move it out of the carousel's lead position. Possible causes: malware entering through comments firewall, happened before; breach of the backdoor's encryption, unlikely; RAT installed in an earlier feed by TRIBE, why would TRIBE do that? Who is messing with me and why?

The Colonel suddenly loses precision, a lack of control clogs his mind. He tries to regroup with the woman he met at a library in Kyoto when the entire world was young.

Her head only came up to his ribs when they hugged. She was small but solid. This tiny woman once in this same garage right over there somehow lifted sheets of falling plywood that would have snapped his shin bone, superhuman will feeding muscle somehow. Not many people possess superhuman will. Some soldiers do. She hated his hardening as he grew older, and she was right but he refused. She had a cocky little smile that said I will beat you at chess. Her face extraordinary. She wrote down on a napkin once he still keeps a little haiku about a sunset from their balcony where they drank wine. The palms of her hands upon you held kindness and strength. Such a playful, alive, handsome woman. Figure it out, Colonel. Love, Li.

CHAPTER CROWD

I believe we're getting into some kind of high-level bullshit here.

The word processor function does not require a connection to anything except a printer three feet away. Trammell writes The Daily Truth on OpenOffice Writer, a decades old free software with enough font options to make the newsletter look serious-minded and organized but not enough to inject a little jazz into its design. That's okay with Trammell. But he wouldn't mind figuring out a way to make the design jump off the library counter and convenience store rack a little more and grab the attention of passersby. Sell them excitement, feed them truth. He will have to ask this Lucy girl if she has any ideas on how to do that.

The Starbucks in St. Augustine seems crowded to Trammell but he has never been to a Starbucks and so isn't sure what constitutes crowded. There are about twenty-five people inside with ghost-lit faces over laptops and lattes and a few wearing headfeed helmets and four or five others with colorful designer thoughtext receivers attached to their temples and there's one having a swordfight or something in the corner wearing VR glasses and not one with a book or a newspaper or a conversation. Trammell spots someone he thinks might be Lucy at a table near the back and she's watching TV, not connected to anything, doesn't see him, not glancing at the door at all. The TV is on Impetus News with a countdown banner that says President Holland press conference is coming in 4:32, 4:31, 4:30, 4:29. The possible Lucy turns her head a little up and toward Trammell, looking at nothing specific, some spot beside the TV above the tables. Ignoring the countdown and pre-statement analysis. Thinking on her own. Good. He walks toward her. She appears to have old eyes on a young face, dusky brown with hints of blue? Not flirty eyes. Serious eyes. Good. As Trammell weaves through the last tables she doesn't look at him until logically warranted. Good. No false brightness. No social niceties bullshit. The unalloyed confidence of the introvert, perhaps. Good.

"Hi, I'm Trammell."

"I figured you were, you were kind of staring at me, checking me out. I'm Lucinda Neale, but I only use that for my byline. You can call me Lucy."

"How did you see me? I was looking at you and you never once looked at me."

"I have my ways. Eyes on the side, like a lizard."

Funny and weird in the first 10 seconds. Good. No handshake, stays seated after a quick half-lift, deals with social ritual as efficiently as possible, an authentic smile instead, slightly buck teeth, not afraid to show them. No makeup or very little. A cute young offbeat girl. A confidence of mind, not of appearance. Freckles on light brown skin. Maybe Irish somewhere in there. Truth is beauty. Good. No thoughttext, no VR glasses, no iWatch, no headfeed. Good, good, good, good. She has a laptop open in front of her.

"People just call me Trammell. Younger reporters used to make fun of me for trying to create a gruff editor persona, but now it's just me and who gives a fuck."

"If you don't mind not using the f-word, I'd appreciate it."

"Uh, sure. Sorry. I always assume people won't be offended, but I'm often wrong."

"I'm not offended, just irritated. Fuck is an overused word."

Trammell laughs and Lucy smiles back.

"Well, I'm not really sure why I'm here. James asked me to help you and I didn't want to because I'm, well, really just an old fart who's pretty much removed from the world and likes it that way. But I have to say I do like you so far."

"You don't even know me."

"A little. Contrary to the old adage, you can judge a book by its cover."

"We'll see if you're right."

Sexy if sex mattered anymore. Good. Nice attribute to have, the flip conversational challenge, speaks to a quick mind, speaks to a reporter's charm and trust. Good.

In the short silence that follows Trammell's mind drifts suddenly back to an earlier part of the conversation and even farther back than that. He changes direction and mood so quickly now in old age, almost feels like a plummet in the middle of an encounter with the outside world. Normalcy sometimes evades him.

"My late wife even used to call me Trammell."

"That's kind of sweet."

"Yes it was, except when she barked it."

"Trammell it is, then. Where do we go next on the port

bombing. I have some ideas."

Good. Back on track. Another of those quick shifts thanks to this Lucy girl. No time really to fuck with stories about your dead wife. No time for a plummet, old man. Good. She's got moxie, if that's still a word.

"Sure, sure. That's why we're here. Don't you want a double latte triple asskicker or something?" His tone with a joke is the same as his tone with everything: worn-out passion.

She laughs impatiently. "No, thank you. I just want to get going on the story. And asskicker is okay, a little more original than fuck but not much. James didn't tell me a lot, gave me the Harold Dumas name you had, said he was looking for a possible old number, said he should be our focus. What did he tell you?"

Trammell feels a warm welling of old energy, talking through a story for the first time in a long time. Lucy looks at him with the same energy but imbued with youth.

"I saw Dumas's name on my neighbor's cellphone, he's a TRIBE member. A text said a very weird thing: 'You do not know Harold Dumas.'"

"Wait a minute. You saying it out loud made me think of something," Lucy breaks in, grabs her phone, finds what she's looking for. "There's a Harold Dumas who's a person of interest in a double shooting in Jacksonville Beach. I got a text about a half hour ago from a detective I know there."

"Really. Holy shit," says Trammell, baggy eyes newly alive. "What is up with this poor guy? I believe we're getting into some kind of high-level bullshit here. Did you read TRIBE's statement yet?"

"Yes, I got it on Twitwit even though I have never had anything to do with TRIBE. Not exactly a black girl's scene. Must have been a bot retweet."

"I've read about but never seen bots. Don't know much about them except that they're insidious shit."

"Yeh, they can be. They multiply the number of likes and retweets with tens of thousands of fake followers until it becomes trending. Russians use it a lot with their fake news. TRIBE apparently too. Everything's fake from start to finish, the original story and the popularity that gives it force."

"That's why I like being old and near death. Time to exit this fake scene, man.

"You just sounded like my father. He used to get into hippie-beatnik mode."

"Must be as old as me."

"He was killed, shot on the street, when I was 13, but don't feel bad. I brought him up."

"I won't. Feel bad, I mean. We all lose someone. Anyway, TRIBE didn't name him in the statement, but this Harold Dumas must be the guy they're saying is the plant from the DNC, with Holland's involvement. Struck me as ludicrous and violently false, just the kind of thing the TRIBE base would believe. For one thing, Dumas is a computer programmer with two kids who apparently has a good heart."

"How do you know that?"

"The name rang a very faint bell in my crapped-out brain and sure enough, James found it in the Times-Picayune archives. Dumas was the IT manager at the Superdome during Katrina, and the story was about how he set up the dome's computer system for the relief operation even though it meant the massive and expensive transfer of Superdome data to other systems. His bosses rejected the idea twice, according to public records, but ol' Harold pressed on. The reporter who did the story was obsessive about her notebooks. James is trying to reach her, see if she has a number. That's the best we have and that's not very good. Will your detective give you a number?"

"Maybe. I'll see." She texts him. "If nothing else he could tell me if Dumas lived in the house where the shootings took place. I could go there, talk to neighbors, see if any investigators I know are on scene."

"You might want to — ," Trammell interrupts himself after Lucy says Shhh to look at the television high on the wall, where President Holland begins her press conference. Aside from shorter but still stylish hair, she is as beautiful as she was when she won an Oscar for "Remember Yesterday Tomorrow."

"First of all, our hearts go out to the families of the four men who died this morning in the terrible and senseless bombing of a cargo ship at the Jacksonville port. We will give them all the help and support they need to get through this. We also will not rest until the perpetrator of this horrific act is captured. We believe and hope that can happen quickly. We have devoted the full resources of the FBI and Homeland Security to this investigation. We have tightened security at all American ports and harbors. However, we do not have any evidence at this time that any other facilities are threatened. We also do not have indications at this time that any outside terrorist group was involved, but that could certainly change as new information comes in. We believe at this time it was an isolated act of domestic terrorism."

"The investigators will follow the facts. What they will not do is consider ridiculous lies coming from my opponent's camp, pulled from thin air. I will not even address them here except to say: I am horrified by this hate-filled violence and will not rest until we find out what happened and who was behind it. Thank you."

President Holland leaves the podium without taking shouted questions and the commentator's voice enters the television noting first that the president did not deny involvement in the bombing.

Risky, whispers Lucy to the television, then says it out loud. "She ignored TRIBE's fake news. Now Hammerschmidt will just double down on it until it becomes embedded in the news cycle."

Trammell nods and smiles inside because it's so nice to see a young person with a slower, deliberative mind.

The detective texts Lucy back. It is indeed Dumas's house, but a rental. He has a cellphone number but it doesn't work and GPS is blocked somehow. The victims were a Michael Wagner and Linda Dumas, Harold's wife. Wagner is dead but she's still alive.

"I'm heading to Jacksonville. This guy's accused of killing, or trying to kill, his own wife for mercy's sake." Lucy googlies Wagner. "Holy Moly. He's the chapter president for TRIBE. So they're saying this Dumas guy infiltrated the group, planned and carried out a bombing to make TRIBE and Hammerschmidt look bad, then tried to murder the local official and his own wife to cover his tracks? I'll head to the house first and see if anyone knows where he might go. Call me if that old number comes through."

"Or you just call James directly. He's the one trying to reach the reporter who might have it. And remember to search the periphery. Look for the smallest details. Talk to the people who aren't obvious, not just the next door neighbors. One of the finest stories written about JFK's assassination was by Jimmy Breslin, on the man who dug the president's grave."

"I've read that. It was good. Thanks for the reminder."

"Is there any reason to go to the port and help the primary guy?"

"I think I'd just be duplicating. He'll interview some of the TRIBE guys if he can get to them. Homeland press guys are pretty much controlling the scene and the information. I'll stay on Dumas."

"You're the boss. I like nodding in agreement much better than instructing. I do think you should do one more thing, though. Call a guy named Rick Something, uh, Smithson, I think, Smith-something, at Southern Poverty Law Center in Montgomery. Mention my name. I wish I could remember his. Anyway, he should still be there, he was a researcher who lived for the work. Ask him or whoever's there to see if any hackers or computer hotshots turn up in TRIBE's Florida's chapter. They keep tabs on cyber hate crimes. What are we forgetting?"

"I can't think of anything right now. And thanks for asking, sign of a good editor, one who doesn't know everything or think he does."

"I'll turn my cell on, which I never do, so give me some time to figure out how to answer it. Call me if you find something. Very nice talking with you, meeting you, Lucy. You seem smart and talented and I would be encouraged about the future if I wasn't so depressed about the future. I'm going over to meet a guy named The Colonel at ironheel.com, the site that released TRIBE's statement, see what he might know. He's only a few miles down the coast from my house. But first I'm going to try to get home for a quick nap or I won't get through the day, so don't call for the next hour or so."

Lucy laughs with mouth agape. "Just don't sleep through the excitement, old man. I'll call James if I can't reach you."

"I also need to check on my cat. He doesn't like being alone."

CHAPTER SCREAM

Nature bats last.

The sound of a chainsaw cutting trees does not reach Norman's ears anymore, but a branch falls on the edge of his vision, and he remembers the sound and his eyes go wide and scared. He remembers the sound deep inside, amputation without anesthesia, the screams of cells. The cutting is next door, the Cantsitstills have hired someone again. They are humans who lack the depth to understand animals and plants. All of the trees in Trammell and Norman's backyard shudder, their fungi excites, their roots send chemical warnings. Norman wishes Trammell was here at a time like this, when he is scared. He is always here by now, lifting his weights or riding his indoor bike thing and then taking his morning nap with Norman before the newsletter work in early afternoon. That is their day and their life and as it should be, not scared-to-death trees and living limbs falling and alone. Norman still sits in the family room. Trammell came but left again, and absence fills him like Karen who never came back. The branch falling to earth would piss Trammell off and send him into one of his plummets or get him ranting. Norman despises Rob and Rhonda Cantsitstill because Trammell despises them. They cut and cut and cut and trim and mow and erase all nature from their property and life. Three types said Da Vinci: Those who see. Those who see when shown. Those who do not see. The Cantsitstills do not see. The do not sees are winning. They fashion river rock and sod and hibiscus into the lawn care version of fake news, little tumors on the larger disease. Trammell used to let loose on the Cantsitstills when Norman could hear. Just thinking about Trammell babbling makes Norman less scared. You tell 'em, Trammell. Another branch crashes and the peripheral horror scares him, but he curls back up into himself into his own little world and whispers to the trees just beyond the glass door: You are safe here. Trammell will keep us safe. Unless Trammell never comes back.

CHAPTER DRIVING

The most effective means of overcoming humanity is to let it out as you go.

Heading back home from Starbucks on the crowded highway:

"There are only three elements required of you to drive responsibly, motherfucker: Be alert, be confident, be consistent with expectations. That's it. A gorilla could learn it in a year of research in Hawaii and you can't learn it in a lifetime. Do not swerve between lanes going ninety in a car built for dirt roads in Kentucky. I'm sure you'll be voting for Hammerfuck, yet another brilliant mind deciding our fucking future. You're not making a heroin run, fucker. Or maybe you are. In any event, you came within three feet of my front bumper and if you had clipped me one or both of us would have somersaulted and flipped ten times into the forest on the shoulder and be dead. I cannot be dead right now because Norman would have no one to take care of him or love him. So you, motherfucker, need to die yourself instead. Maybe a mile or two down the road. I'll be looking for you. Just don't kill anyone else and don't block the highway until I get past. I'll call 911 for you. Tell them all about your driving record."

A mile or two later:

"Wood storks feeding in the ditch beside the interstate fills one with the sense that wood storks feed in the ditch beside the interstate."

Less than a mile later:

"Let me get past you, let me get past you, do not veer, do not see what is not there, please do see what is there: Me getting past you, driving past you, let me get past you. Fucking driverless truck."

Quarter mile later:

"And, we hit the Bermuda Triangle of I-95. I was actually listening to NPR, one of the few times they don't have Tchaikovsky or some other ancient music on. Better tell him the news. But today, on this day, all I want to do is listen to your wonderful vital news programming. However I can't if you don't send out a signal strong enough to get through a foggy day. I know it's not completely your fault, with two thousand fucking cell and headfeed towers between you and me. But you're fine in rain. Why wouldn't fog be the same heavy air? I can see a sunny day, when thousands of signals stream unimpeded through blue sky, bumping and grinding with each other, but fog should be a great conductor. Does it weigh on the signal too heavily, dropping it down to a smaller radius? My physics is not sound. Anyway, you are forcing me to turn you off, and I'm not going to donate anything until you learn to work in the fog and the sun."

Coming upon packed interstate vehicles weaving and bobbing:

"Ah, the always welcome Army convoy. Saving taxpayer dollars by going fucking 50 on the interstate and disrupting traffic for miles. Like the green, though, really like the green."

Just past the convoy:

Karen Trammell, MISSING. Look again at the poster on the back of the truck. Read it out loud.

"Carol Hammond, MISSING."

Several miles of silence later:

"What do you think, K? I'm a little worried about Lucy. I have no idea what to expect of this guy Dumas. I don't think he's one of those Hammer primitives, just desperate and scared. His heart seemed in a good place in that old article we found, but hearts can harden. Look at mine for God's sake. Anyway, Lucy seems to be able to take care of herself. She's a smart little twenty-something, self-contained, an observer. Rare bird, and cute as can be in her confidence. I think you'd like her."

Passes a pickup with bumper stickers endorsing the nation's destruction by weapons of mass stupidity.

"Yeh, boy, there goes John Bobby Bubba Conroy, white dude in a pickup wants to Bring Down The Hammer! Destroying the country one dumbshit at a time. Learn how to think, motherfucker. That's why your life sucks. Quit taking it out on the rest of us."

And so on and etcetera rolling down the highway. He forgets to take the exit for home, apologizes to Norman, takes another caffeine pill from the ones he keeps in the car, continues the four miles to The Colonel's massive oceanfront home, talks and rants, old bearded bubblehead alone going seventy. Karen stopped riding with Trammell unless she absolutely had to a year or so before she died, but he still talks to her about things when he's driving around.

Trammell's cellphone rings and after three failed attempts he manages to push the right button and answer it: James calling with an interview, can he do it, the wife of one of the workers killed.

CHAPTER DOUBT

At first I was nervous, but then I let the talent take over.

You are third-person, Lucy tells herself, her routine mantra, as she drives north to find Harold Dumas somewhere in Jacksonville Beach. Her non-reporter friends think her third-person mind game is weird, but it isn't, just a different road to confidence and empathy, any reporter's two essential traits. Good ones like Lucy pull out honesty and insight because they can leave their own lives for a while and exist in the third-person world of the interview. Ignore the personal. It has no bearing on the task at hand. It's the only way to see the other person's mind clearly. Her mother, Dana Neale, now retired, was an investigator with the Duval County Sheriff's Office who rose in the ranks alongside men. She approached cases and interviews in the same way. Step back, move forward: The work, the suspect, the crime and the next move are in front of you. When Lucy's father was killed, her mother reinforced the notion and its importance to her future — she saw it as a means of resolve, a crusher of doubt, a check on anger and grief. Lucy was thirteen, a horrible time for him to leave. There is no good time for a father to die, of course, but Lucy wasn't ready at all and of course not the way he died. She was very smart but also very small and not yet determined enough. He told her several times over his last year that she could be "magnificent" as she readied to enter high school, and she didn't believe him so much as trust implicitly that he believed it himself. He had an Irish soul and faith in his children's abilities. Her mother was more objective, less romantic, but she missed Lucy's father deeply, and sharpened the notion of a third-person life in overcoming her own sadness. Neither of them understands his killer to this day, cannot comprehend random hatred, specific hatred, a single act so infuriating that he killed. He could have shouted, spit on him, beat him up. But he killed. He God Almighty killed. Dana's love for Lucy is objective and embedded. Lucy calls her as she drives.

"Mom, whatcha' doing?"

"Driving to the store to get some milk. What's wrong? Is something wrong in your new job?"

"Not wrong, just a little weird and a really huge story and I'm having trouble getting into the third-person. We're covering the bombing at the port and I'm driving to Jacksonville Beach pretty much on my own to try to find a suspected terrorist bomber and murderer who's a member of TRIBE. I'm kind of freakin' out. Not too confident."

"You know what to do, baby. Keep it precise. Every step precise. 'Not too confident' is part of the equation. Don't get ahead of yourself, don't wallow in the muddy stuff. If you're concentrating, letting the talent and skill do the work, you won't second-guess and you won't doubt. Keeps you alert too. And you know of course, I don't have to tell you, be careful around any TRIBE guys. A lot of them will hate you the minute they see you. Just like the one who killed Dad."

"I know, Mom, but I don't think the guy I'm looking for is a hardcore racist. The main thing I'm worrying about is preparation. I feel a little like an amateur, a newbie. You know I like to be prepared because that's my job. But on this story I don't have anything to be precise about. I just talked with an old retired editor that my boss hooked me up with and he was virtually no help. 'Search the periphery' and 'look for the smallest detail' was his sage advice. Afterward he was going home to take a nap and feed his cat or something. I don't have any leads really except whatever else I might get from your old partner. He didn't have much when I called him."

"How is he?"

"He seems good, seems okay. He says to tell you hello and that his new partner sucks compared to you. He's not on this case but he's familiar with it and will dig a little more for me. I got my best stuff from a Jax Beach investigator I know. They've got one guy who's a person of interest in a double shooting named Harold Dumas, and he's the guy I'm trying to find because he's somehow connected to the bombing too. So I'm just heading to his house, which is now a crime scene, and seeing what I can find from neighbors. Search the periphery, I guess. CNN just reported the name was sent out to all TRIBE chapters, but I don't think anyone has what I have on the double shootings, the Dumas connection there, unless local TV got it from neighbors. They're pretty much all out at the port. I talked to my editor in Washington and he wants me to file something on the shootings as quick as I can but not too quick. After I've gotten what I can from the scene. We've already reported the name related to TRIBE and the bombing, before CNN did. The

FBI is all over it looking for him, of course, but haven't said anything publicly yet. I'm sure they'll be at his house. Fortunately Jax Beach hasn't put a BOLO out on him for the shootings. Jurisdiction war, I'm sure. And Dumas rents the house, so property records won't show where he lives. Could slow down the other media a bit, and I don't think CNN or any of the big boys have connected the dots on the name yet. Except me."

"That's my girl."

"Gotta go, Mom. Pulling into the neighborhood. The work is in front of me. Go get your milk. Talk to you soon. I love you in the way that I love you."

The laughter of her mom on a notion that would make other mothers cry gives Lucy a little boost as she parks her Mini on the street just outside the crime scene tape and steps out into the murder investigation swarming with deputies and forensic and FBI guys. No TV crews yet, too busy at the bombing, and she has the scene alone except for a reporter she knows from the Times-Union's bureau. She's not very good, but Lucy still knows to watch what she says. Walking toward the yellow crime scene tape life gently, intellectually comes alive.

CHAPTER KNIVES

Let's see what they're reporting about this on state TV.

Welcome back from break, students. If you read your workshop summary, as I trust you did, you know that the free press often aligns with authoritarians. Fux News and ironheel.com are recent examples, endorsing a series of self-proclaimed 'strong men' for president because it appeals to angry and aggrieved white people, who make up a large and ever-growing slice of the media marketplace. The angry are more passionate and loyal than the comfortable, and media executives and their star performers know it. But such alliances are nothing new. Just as the New York World and Journal battled for profits and power with sensational stories that helped start the Spanish-American War, some newspapers openly promoted ideologies as a means of forming alliances and motivating their core subscribers. These strategies often went well beyond opinion pieces or editorial stances by presenting these beliefs as legitimate news coverage. This was commonplace before and after the Golden Age of the Watergate era, but never quite so brazen as when a British newspaper cheered on the dictator that would later kill hundreds of thousands of British boys. In the 1930s, the Daily Mail in London supported Nazism when it was on the rise and becoming more ruthless in Germany. The publisher, Lord Rothemere, was friends with Adolph Hitler and Benito Mussolini, and his audience was primarily older working class nationalists who one competing newspaper described as "people unaccustomed to thinking."

Here was the newspaper's response on July 2, 1934 to The Night of the Long Knives, when Hitler's SS troops arrested and executed dozens of officials from a rival military group seen as a threat:

"Herr Adolph Hitler, the German Chancellor, has saved his country. Swiftly and with exorable severity, he has delivered Germany from men who had become a danger to the unity of the German people and to the order of the state. With lightning rapidity he has caused them to be removed from high office, to be arrested, and put to death.

"The names of the men who have been shot by his orders are already known. Hitler's love of Germany has triumphed over private friendships and fidelity to comrades who had stood shoulder to shoulder with him in the fight for Germany's future."

This was not the first time mass executions would be portrayed as an honorable truth, of course. To list the examples would take up an entire class session, I'm afraid.

CHAPTER SIDEBAR

That's my husband getting those damn ratings.

He was killed immediately, Janice Maloney hopes with hate underneath.

"Did that help in any way? I mean, the fact that he didn't suffer?"

"No. Not really. No. I'd rather he have suffered and still been here. That's not my Billy sitting there. I mean I'm glad if he didn't suffer, but nothing really feels different inside. I can tell you what I felt most of all right away. Anger. That CNN would run it. Would put something so horrible on the television just for ratings. That's my husband getting those damn ratings. That's why I called you people. I don't want to talk a lot more about it, but I want you to run this photo of him."

Trammell takes the photo. Billy is sitting on a porch swing with a young tomboy-looking girl beside him.

"Granddaughter?"

Mrs. Maloney nods her head yes. "Jessica. She loved her granddad, and Billy loved being a granddad. I don't know what she's going to do."

The love of memory and a shattered life share the same face.

"It's a real nice photo. I'll be sure it gets to the editor I'm working with on this. I don't know computers very well and don't have a legitimate cellphone, so I can't send it to him right now. But I will."

"Let me see the photo." She acts like a mother to a man

twenty years older than her and it lifts her a little from the depths of grief. “You are an old dinosaur, aren’t you? Why does a big deal like the Truth Network have some old-timer like you covering this big a story, if you don’t mind my asking.”

Trammell laughs. “The editor in Washington was an old reporter of mine. He just needed me in a pinch. We have a very good young reporter working the main story.”

“Well, thank goodness for that” and she let out a little laugh like a hiccup.

“Is that the first time you’ve laughed today?”

“Yes it is. Yes it is.” Her face drops back to emptiness. “What’s the fella’s number in Washington?” She takes a picture of the photo with her phone. Trammell gives her the number and she sends a text with the photo of Billy and Jessica, then puts the photo back on the dining room table.

Trammell says “I should send him a photo of you, too.”

“I don’t want that. Just Billy and Jessica.”

“The people who read your story need to put a voice to a face. It helps them understand the story better. It’s not meant to exploit you.”

“That’s just so much bullshit.”

“You’re right to a certain extent. But what I said is true, too.”

“Allright. I know I don’t look good, but I guess I’m not supposed to look good. Go ahead.”

Trammell takes three shots with Mrs. Maloney’s phone and she’s okay with the third one and sends it to James in Washington.

"Thank you." She nods you're welcome. Trammell leans back and positions his notebook on his knee.

"I don't really want to talk anymore. Just use the photo, please." She gets up to show Trammell out.

"Please wait. I can't write this without you telling me what kind of man, what kind of husband, what kind of grandfather Billy was. I just can't. It wouldn't be fair to him."

She stands silent for a moment and then sits back down. "That's a line of bullshit, too."

"It's not, really. You're wrong about that. Reporters aren't Satan. Tell me about him. Honor him," Trammell says. They talk for ten more minutes and Trammell leaves. He sits in his car and writes in his notebook for 20 minutes, then calls James.

"You're going to dictate it to me, Trammell?"

"Yes, pretend it's 1980. Here it is. And you should already have the photos. No video. I didn't shoot video. My phone doesn't shoot video. Here's the sidebar. I can flesh it out a little and make it better later if you want. Haven't done this in a while. Here goes."

"(Lede) Billy Maloney was sitting in the driver's seat of a brand new Toyota Brigadier when the bomb went off and blew a hole in the hull five feet away. He was just doing his job, getting the SUVs ready for unloading, when the explosion incinerated him.

"(new graf) No one called Janice Maloney to let her know that her husband was among the four dead workers in Saturday's bombing of an NYK cargo ship. She found out from the TV news when she saw a cellphone video taken by a coworker who was the first to arrive on the scene.

"(new graf) In the video, Billy's body was still sitting inside the charred silver Brigadier on the starboard side of the hold. The SUV was crumpled and upended onto its side by the blast that left a 20-foot hole of tongued metal bent inward in the hull. Blue sky and the Port of Jacksonville can be seen through the hole.

"(new graf) A piece of blue cloth on the worker's chest made Janice Maloney gasp and she knew right then that the worst thing possible in her life had happened.

"(new graf) Janice's voice trembles three hours later. (quote) "He always carried a blue handkerchief in his shirt pocket, and that's how I knew it was him." (close quote.)

"(new graf) CNN obtained the video and credited the worker by name. The network warned viewers beforehand that it was shocking and graphic.

"(quote) "He sweated a lot and needed it to keep the sweat out of his eyes," Janice says. "He worked as a cargo specialist for NYK Shipping and spent most of his time in the holds of massive ships, which can get hot, getting cars like Toyotas and Lexuses ready for unloading, the interior things like the bluetooth and GPS and that stuff, getting them all ready to be unloaded."

"(new graf) The coworker who shot the video held his cellphone in one hand while trying with the other hand to peel the car seat's protective covering off of Billy's body where it had melted around him and merged with his body and clothes. It's not clear if the coworker was trying to help and possibly see if Billy could still be alive or if he was just trying to get a clearer shot of him.

"(new graf) The shredded piece of blue handkerchief somehow remained intact inside the melted plastic and still clung to the chest of Billy's burnt body.

"(new graf. quote) "They had no right. The worker had no right and then CNN had no right to run it. I didn't need to see Billy like that and didn't need to find out that way and now the whole damn world has seen my Billy that way." (close quote)

"(new graf) Janice sits on the edge of a dining room chair in the St. Augustine home where she and Billy have lived for 32 years. Her hands clasp her knees for support and she stares at the floor. Eye makeup and tears have dried on her cheeks. Her anger will not ease, but she talks about Billy quietly and firmly.

"(new graf, quote) "I knew he was working Brigadiers this morning 'cause he joked about it, said 'We oughta look into one of these.' Of course we could never afford it. But that's what left me with no doubt at all that it was my Billy sitting there. I saw the blue on his chest and the announcer said they were Brigadiers." (close quote)

"(new graf) Janice shakes her head looking over at a photograph of Billy with the grandchild he dearly loved, who dearly loved him back. Her name is Jessica and she has the look of a little rough-and-tumble tomboy, wearing jeans and a flannel shirt, sitting on granddad's knee.

"(new graf) "I don't know what Jessica is going to do. And I don't know how to tell her. She's only six."

"(new graf) Janice ends the interview politely after that and says "Please leave" to the reporter and the house falls quiet. Billy Maloney was 56. (end of story)"

"Got it?"

"Yes. I now have the first story dictated verbally over a phone in thirty years. I'll check for typos. You were reading pretty fast. It's good, Trammell. Thanks. Looking it over, though, I'm wondering if her finding out first from the video should be the lede, and do you really want to insert the reporter at the end?"

"I thought about that for the lede, too, but I kind of like putting the horror of what she saw first and then juxtaposing her anger and grief with the callousness of the coworker and CNN. As far as inserting myself, you can change it or take it out if you like. I just liked the 'please leave' and wanted to emphasize her aloneness inside the house."

"Yes, yes. I agree with both points. I'm leaving them as is. What about CNN? We need at least a 'did not respond.'"

"You'll need to call them. Add what they give you somewhere near the CNN graf without mucking up the flow too much. I trust you. Also, I didn't get into anything about Maloney's relationship to TRIBE. Janice said he used to be a member but in the last couple of years, since Hammerschmidt announced, really, they'd been giving him a hard time, calling him a Jap lover and ridiculous shit like that. It just didn't fit in this. Maybe you can use it in your main bar. Probably won't fit in Lucy's story on Dumas. She seems good, James, quiet smart, the best kind. I'll send you a feed on the Maloney TRIBE stuff when I get home. I didn't get my nap today and didn't check on Norman, all for you, James. I'm popping another caffeine pill and going to The Colonel's house now."

"Good luck. Hope it's not a dead end. Oh, and guess what? Believe it or not, Sheri texted me back and she still had the number of a Harold Dumas in her cloud archive. Found it in a few minutes. I called the number but got no answer. Was a long shot, anyway, but a good one. I'll give it to Lucy and she can try again."

CHAPTER SOMEONE

Although advertising agencies often use mixed race couples in their television and social media commercials to reflect the sensibilities of young consumers and get a 2-for-1 bargain in their demographic targeting, the message is seen as Jew-controlled motherfucking Hollywood bullshit by a big chunk of America.

Hostility stares at Lucy walking toward it.

"What are you, some kind of reporter?" says the maintenance guy, Clayton on his shirt, maybe mid-thirties with rough tanned skin, at the pool down the street from Harold's crime scene house while Lucy is still thirty feet away from him. "Lamestream fake news?"

"Oh, God, you're one of those people," says Lucy, non-threatening, a friendly, freckled smile. Her small stature and young face help diffuse situations sometimes. "TRIBE?"

"Yep, a proud member. Can I help you with something, or maybe not help you with something, depending on what you ask." He leans on the white railing that surrounds the pool and divides the two of them. It is an old pool in an old development once marketed as affordable paradise. Lucy hates his look, dullness made alive by anger, the only confidence he knows, but she focuses on his eyes to overcome the feeling. They are blue, like her dad's. Somewhere in their pale emptiness appears to be kindness.

"My name is Lucy Neale and I work for Truth Network."

Kindness retreats. "I hate fucking Truth Network."

"Well, that's your prerogative, Clayton. I'm just trying to find out the truth, as the name implies."

"Or whatever so-called truth that lays into Hammer, right? Look until you find it, anonymous sources, right, and tell lies about him even if your sources won't lie for you. Right? You guys just can't handle a real leader. Lies Network is more like it."

Lucy looks down, closes her notebook. "I guess all this means you don't want to talk to me."

"Damn straight. What'd you want to ask, anyway?"

"Just hoping you might know Harold Dumas. He's the one who lives up the street where two people were—"

"I know Harold. He's a pretty good guy, with a fat wife whose name I can't remember. I know him a little. Not really one of us, kind of an asshole, really, thinks he's smarter than you, but he's okay. Don't quote any of that. Don't quote me. And I didn't mean anything by the fat wife thing. My wife's a little overweight too and she's still a good woman. What'd you want to know about him?"

Kindness falls back into his eyes. Lucy proceeds gently as if two humans are having a conversation.

"Well, I was looking around his house just now, and they keep their yards pretty immaculate, so a piece of paper blowing in the wind stood out in the bushes next door. It was a flier from the library, and it had been mailed to Harold Dumas. So I'm wondering if you might know anything about that or where he might go if the cops were after him."

"Well, that's some pretty good observation, little lady. Harold just happens to go to the library first thing every Saturday to work on some kind of research he's doing, I don't know what, but he's a computer genius – just ask him – so it must have something to do with that. I think he mentioned drones once, and I've seen him flying one around here before. I'm sure he's not there with all this shit going on, but that's where he'd normally be on a Saturday morning, always really early, just when I'm getting into work. We cross paths sometimes. He's talked to me about it like in secret, but since I don't really like him that much, I'm okay telling you."

"Just don't tell anyone else." Lucy smiles and winks at him before turning to leave. "I want the scoop of an interview with him."

"Deal," says Clayton, winking back, looking happier now over his entire face, as if he sort of fits in with the smarter world and this young smart black girl sort of likes him.

CHAPTER SOMEONE

We remain staff members at the research station and remain committed to the pursuit of truth.

Harold has entered the Realm of Knowledge and Silence, or so says faded magic marker lettering on a cardboard box flap thumbtacked to a skinny pine tree beside the pine-needle-and-leaf-strewn clearing in the woods behind the library. First laugh Harold's had today. The Realm holds no special properties that he can ascertain beyond stillness, downtrodden life, wet leaves and dripping fog. No one is here that he can see. Harold sits on a turned-over milk crate, laptop on his knees, the detritus of the homeless scattered all around him: cellophane wrappers, fast food sacks, cigarette butts, whiskey bottles, beer cans, wet blankets, filth, mud, an absence of any human dignity. Four tents, two folded lawn chairs leaning against a tree, other milk crates upside down in a ragged circle around leaves and dirt like a council gathering site. They are the only friends they have, often becoming enemies. None of them are here but it feels like they are. He knows many of them by sight: the black woman of indeterminate age who sleeps covered by a hoodie in the library's back corner near the magazines; the deaf Italian-looking guy who might have been a Tony Bennett-style nightclub singer once somewhere in Harold's imagination; the wiry short redneck white guy Iraq veteran who spends afternoons holding a cardboard plea begging at the main intersection; the overweight young nerdy guy who doesn't seem homeless and stays inside the library on a computer most of the time. Other regulars come and go, never talking of Michelangelo. Harold views these people most days as the lowest form of mediocrity but somehow feels at home here now, cradled in their hideaway within the rush of circumstances, the anarchy his life has so suddenly become. He did not know where else to go. He needed computer access, and the homeless camp close to the library offered that, albeit with the smell of unbathed wet humans. Their B.O. and mildewed hope cling to leaves, bark and fog. He entered the camp cautiously, making sure no one saw him walk down the narrow path, his laptop clutched against his chest, tromping on wet leaves and lowering his head to miss dripping branches and vines. The Realm of Knowledge and Silence sign calmed him and then that feeling went wildly astray when the overweight nerdy guy in tank top with hairy shoulders, cargo shorts and black socks and sandals scared the shit out of him emerging from one of the tents.

"Pretty cool, huh," he said after seeing Harold looking at the sign. He finished off a beer and threw the can in the pile under the sign. "Relax, man. Sorry I scared you. It was a sign on an old research station in Tanzania that closed down after the Germans and then the British abandoned it, and a staff of Tanzanians, I guess you'd call them, still worked there, waiting for their return. The sign on the wall was covered in vines and mold with an old rusted fan on the floor. An incredible photo in National Geographic."

He did not appear dangerous, but this is a homeless camp after all, Harold thinks, and desperation is just boxed-in violence waiting to break out. This guy could get five or six hundred bucks or more for the laptop. Harold caught his breath and tried to speak as if not concerned, fried with fear though he was.

"Yeh, that's pretty cool. I've never heard that phrase before. It actually helped me today. I don't mean to intrude on your space, but I needed a quiet place."

The overweight guy said Help yourself, we don't need reservations, and started hanging clothes on the branches of a dead tree to dry turning his head around to talk as he did. He looked at Harold's computer as if longing for a former life, and indeed that was the case.

"I used to repair those."

"Really. I sell and repair them myself. Or used to, I guess. I got hacked and I'm trying to figure out how."

"Why are you doing that here? I know why I'm here."

"I've got no place else —" Harold caught himself and stuttered "I mean," then said:

"I need to concentrate. Kids always yakking their heads off in the library, so I'm just using their wifi out here."

"The fog and the wet can give you trouble if you're out here long. But I guess you know that."

"Yeh. I'm hoping I can figure it out pretty quickly and move on. Thanks."

"Look for a RAT. A remote access tool."

"I know what it is. I already have. Can't find one. Can't find any altered code anywhere."

"Sometimes they hide them in plain sight. Check all of your

routine programs like Adobe and Word for any irregularities. One thing to look for is a slash that's been altered. Could be a disguised comma that only existed for a few seconds. That's an old trick that hasn't been used for a long time, since my dad was building video games at least. Someone tried it on him. Maybe one of these young hackers is trying to resurrect it. The way it works is that the comma triggers an alert in the protection software and creates a backup for about thirty seconds that you can snatch, alter and then later replace the original with the hacked version. Don't know if it still works or if they've designed in countermeasures."

"I never knew about that one, before my time I guess. I'll check it out. Thanks. My name's Harold."

"My name's Harold, too. Harold Nolastname, I've decided. Good luck, man. I'm going inside to get cool and dry. Take it easy out here and don't mess with Smitty, the little wiry redneck guy. He's got a little PTSD going. He's out at the intersection now working, but just be careful around him when he gets back."

"Will do. Thanks for your help, Harold Nolastname."

"Hope you find your hack."

Harold checks code for the next half-hour alone in the camp and is about halfway through with everything looking normal, all of it fucking normal. He buries his face in his hands and rubs his eyes, and doing so makes the world disappear in a fake frantic not-true way. Two things happen in quick succession to shatter Harold's fake cocoon: 1) His personal cellphone rings, his old flip-top, how could anyone have the number, only Linda has that number, impossible but then, impossible has no boundary anymore, and 2) Someone new is brushing through branches and palmettos approaching on the path.

CHAPTER SOMEONE

A little nugget of revenge is all most men need.

James Dunbar in his cluttered little Truth Network office just off K Street gets a call from an unknown number and knows who it is, he hopes.

"James, this is Inconsequential Man."

"Was hoping it was you. What's new?"

"Everything is new. All of this is on background and I'm not even an anonymous source. I might have a couple of recordings you could use if you're a good boy. Agreed?"

"I'm listening."

"You saw this morning's statement, right?"

"Yep. Bullshit, I assumed. Does your base really believe President Holland is behind this?"

"Don't denigrate your source, James. I believe in the cause but not the consequences. Four dead American workers. That's the only reason I'm calling you."

"So Maestro finally went too far for even you?"

"Ditto what I just said, asshole. Do you want what I have or not?"

"Yes, of course. I'm just the smartass liberal media."

"You certainly fucking are. (laughs) Let's get on with this. First, as you guessed, a DNC-slash-Holland plant in TRIBE setting off the bomb is indeed bullshit and Harold Dumas is nothing but a fall guy."

"How did you know I had Harold Dumas's name?"

"I just know. It's only a matter of time before everyone knows it. Maestro wants them to, or did. He's acting stranger now, not moving on this like he normally would. But he had me send out that text message earlier to all TRIBE members that your old friend down in Florida saw."

"How did you know about Trammell, for God's sake?"

"As stated, I just know. I do all the cybersecurity checks in Maestro's office before he comes in each day — his phone, his surveillance feed, everything — so I just know. I tell you this only to ensure you that this is reliable information."

"Thanks for that."

"Anyway, something clicked this morning after that statement and I looked back in the phone archives I keep just for myself. Just in case. Anyway, Maestro made a call last year, several calls really, that you'll be interested in. Have you ever heard of a guy named Mike Wagner?

"Yes. I'm familiar with the name. My reporter is working several angles. We haven't reported anything on Wagner yet, but I know he was the local TRIBE chapter president."

"He's also dead. Did you know that?"

"Yes, I knew. But I wasn't saying anything until I knew what you knew. Wagner was one of the people killed this morning in a double shooting in Jacksonville Beach."

"That shouldn't surprise you if you listen to these tapes. Maestro was hatching something with Wagner more than a year ago. Wagner says more than Maestro, kind of going over a checklist. He mentions Dumas, and his research into drones, and he mentions Dumas's wife. She was a key. They don't say why, but I'm guessing they needed her for access to Dumas and his computer. They don't say much more than that incriminating on the first tape."

"And on the second?"

"Maestro hung up the first call that he took in the office and went somewhere else to call him back. Maestro doesn't know that I monitor his personal phone. He buys a new prepaid one every couple of weeks but I copy the one he's using every Friday. Fucker doesn't suspect a thing. Anyway, the second call to Wagner is where the really interesting stuff comes out. I'm not saying anything more on this line. You'll have to listen for yourself. I'm sending you other calls he made on his personal phone, too, to some of the new money and the old money. That's all I'll say on the phone. I want to send them all to you on the dark web, on an encrypted site. Do you have someone who can access the dark web?"

"I'll find someone."

"When you do, have that person go to a site called TRIBEunderground under the code AH 88 14 and search Reptilian Chocolate. Only one link will come up. Click on that. Get in with the password 1inconsequentialman! That's where you'll find the phone tapes. After you retrieve them the link will disappear, so make sure you get someone who knows what they're doing. I'm not calling back. Good luck fucking Maestro up the ass."

CHAPTER 9TH WARD

She served in the unknown.

Thin fear animates Lucy walking down the path through the woods behind the Jacksonville Beach library, the tension of wanting to and not wanting to walk down this path. More than data, more than writing, the fear is what she likes best about investigative reporting, at it only three years but she dug this aspect from the beginning, as her Irish hippie father would say, bringing a little smile continuing down the path. The fear of strangers and places never been — a biker bar, a dealer's apartment, an attorney's private country club — talking to other worlds, finding humans there. She digs being afraid. Everything in front of her.

There he sits, has to be him, seen through skinny pines where the path curves, and he's looking right at her. Lucy does not stop and walks into the small clearing of tents and trash and the mean-faced white man sitting on a milk carton with a computer. His mean face holds concentrated fear. She holds her reporter's notebook up like a flag of peace. The man gets nervous, closes his laptop.

"Are you Harold Dumas? I'm Lucy Neale, a reporter for Truth Network."

"I don't know you and don't want to talk to you. And why should I believe you are who you say you are?"

"You can call my editor if you like. I'm brand new. Don't have any cards or ID yet. I just want to get your side on all of this, the bombing, the shooting at your house. I can conceal whatever we need to conceal to protect your location."

"How did you find me?"

"So you are Harold Dumas?"

"Maybe. But I need you to assure me you won't fuck me over. I am being fucked right and left. Everyone is apparently looking for me. Someone just fucking called my phone that no one knows except my wife. Was it you? How did you find me?"

"My guess is it was my editor in Washington or an older editor I'm working with. One of them will probably call me next. Believe it or not, I think he got it from a reporter who did a story on you years ago, at the Superdome during Katrina. You must keep your phone a long time."

"Just this one. Nobody has anything on it digitally. It's just for me and my wife. Why the hell would a reporter keep someone's phone number from that many years ago? God almighty, you can't even get free using an obsolete phone."

"Obsessive compulsive. All the best reporters are. Pure luck for us. Or maybe you make your own luck." She thought of Trammell's advice, the periphery, the smallest detail. "I was getting nowhere with investigators at the scene — your entire house and yard are swarming with investigators — and none of the neighbors knew where you might be or wouldn't talk to me to begin with. Then I saw a piece of trash in the flower bed across the street from your house, and for some reason I went over and looked at it, and it was a flier from this library addressed to you. So I came here just in case."

"Did you tell anyone I was here?"

"Not a soul. Although Clayton, your pool maintenance guy,

talked to me for a minute and may know. He said you came here every Saturday. But I doubt if anyone else will talk to him. Unless Jimmy Breslin has risen from the dead."

"What are you talking about?"

"Sorry. Journalism humor. Anyway, I came straight here. Haven't even been inside the library. Haven't confirmed anything with my editor, but he knows I was headed here. He won't say a word."

"He better fucking not. That notice must have fallen out of my pocket. I was hiding over there. You know I didn't do any of this shit. I watched my wife get shot for God's sake."

"You're the prime suspect, just a person of interest for now."

"I guessed as much. My house, my wife, the Mike guy she must be having an affair with. They have me connected to this TRIBE bombing too for God's sake. So I'm sitting down here with the bottom feeders trying to figure out how the fuck someone hijacked my computer and my project. I'm sure that's why they're setting me up, the research I was doing."

"What kind of research? Did someone steal it? The people setting you up?"

"I don't— I don't fucking know. Damn! I'm about to gag down here. God, it stinks. Sometimes these people come into the library and a whole corner of the place smells like mildewed tennis shoes. Just no dignity at all. No self pride."

A new voice appears, a deep woman's voice.

"You didn't used to be an asshole, Harold."

"What the fuck! Who's there?"

The voice came from inside one of the tents but no one emerges. Harold looks over at the tent with timorous hard eyes, and Lucy takes one step back and turns toward the voice, holding her notebook ready. Then ahead of the voice, the grumble of a dog.

"It's okay, Niko, it's okay. I'm someone you knew a long time ago, Harold. Didn't really know, but helped. I recognize your voice. There's a little Zydecko in it. Don't hear that too much in white boys around here."

"Where? When? How do you know me?"

"Doesn't matter too much really. I was just laying down in here listening to you all this time unbeknownst to you and remembered your voice. It finally came to me. Let's just say you weren't an asshole then. You cared about me and the other people. It was in the Superdome. Before during after the flood."

"Who are you? I didn't mean anything by any of it. You're right. I am more of an asshole now. You get older and the world always gets worse instead of better."

"I'm sure you've had it rough, Harold."

"How do you know my name? And yeh, life's kind of rough at the moment. I'm a suspect in a murder and terrorist bombing."

"Well, I guess you got me beat." The voice laughs a deep laugh moan.

"Why don't you come out," Lucy says.

"And who are you?"

"I'm Lucy, a reporter. Trying to get Harold's side of the story."

"Well, I can tell you one side of his story. This man took me and my son into his home after Katrina, and that's the only way I could have moved on."

"Cassandra! You're Cassandra? I remember you! Same name as the actress back then and now the president. That's how I remembered your name among those thousands of people. God, that was a long time ago. Come out, please. I could use a friend."

"Nope, I'm not coming out, Harold. We were only three-week friends but friends I guess just the same. Those three weeks saved me and my boy. It wasn't the flood that got me so much as the son-of-a-bitch I was married to. The flood just made him hit me harder. Then I find a new man and move here and the same thing, the same goddamn thing. I'm not afraid of anything anymore. I'm just not coming out. I was beaten before the flood and beaten after it, and the only thing that changed was location. Now I am free of all that shit and I've got a place here with Niko. I'm the accountant and I guess you'd say the operations manager. I keep up with the intersection money and the shopping center money. It ain't perfect, everybody keeps most of it for themselves, but we've always got a little pot for an emergency. Like a bottle of wine on New Years. We've got sort of an agreement with the library staff. Cops don't bother us. We stay hidden in our own little world. Best place to be."

"The Realm of Knowledge and Silence."

"I didn't put that up there, but yeah."

CHAPTER SOMEONE

I would put a 720 Gazelle Flip in the very advanced category, high risk high reward, and I just don't know if I've gotten good enough to land it yet, but I'll never know if I don't try.

Your life could be destroyed. Can you do it without getting caught. Weigh everything. Weigh MJ. Weigh Marl. Will they be harmed. You don't matter. They do. What will happen if you do it, what will happen if you don't. Nothing to compare any of this to.

Malcolm sits alone in the surveillance room. Bobby left at 7 and is with Jen now helping her not hurt so much and Wilbur called in sick again probably hung over. Four screens to monitor three hours to go. Things are easier on the work end because the reporter Lucy and the fugitive computer guy Harold are together in a library homeless camp, and the old man Trammell and the ironheel guy The Colonel are together in The Colonel's garage where ironheel originates from. So it's really down to two screens but it's not what he's seeing now that pulls on Malcolm's mind like a grave but instead what he saw on Bobby's history when he was trying to get up to speed.

Weigh everything.

You will be discovered and you will be fired. You will be ruined beyond that. Blacklisted in your field. Black guys don't get here too often anyway. You might bring Bobby down with you and how would he pay for Jen's medical. You might put MJ and Marl through absolute hell. Media will camp outside your house if your identity is leaked. You have no reason to trust this reporter Lucy.

Your identity may come out at trial. You may have to testify. You might be charged. Obstruction or accessory or something. Your life may even be at risk. Malcolm Jr.'s and Marl's lives may be at risk. How far up does this go?

You will not be discovered and must sustain the lie forever. You are using a burner phone. The transfer of data will be recorded but if you send the files back to Bobby's system with updated summaries at the same time it will be seen as routine. No one will red-flag a simple routine update and transfer. You will free an innocent man. Good god there's that. You will help convict a person who blew up a ship and killed four men. But nothing's certain. You could be doing this for nothing. Taking this risk for nothing. You have video of a man not Harold entering the back door. He is not identifiable as the shooter but might be. Wispy hair sticking out of the hoodie. The Harold guy is nearly bald. You have audio of a phone call. The murderer just before the murders whispers "Colonel? Colonel?" and the voice answers "This is not The Colonel. Do not call again." There is a chance you will link some unknown higher-up to the murder. Voice recognition might work, but how would a reporter get access to that. Lucy's mom was a cop. She might, she just might. That would be sweet and pure and possibly worth it.

Weigh everything. Malcolm leans back in his chair and tension circulates dissipates through his muscles. He thinks he has decided what to do but needs to talk to his son first. He picks up the burner phone and calls home.

"Hey, MJ. How's your arm?"

"Hurts a little. Kind of a dull throb. I've already been back on my board today."

"Don't overdo it. No flips, no big air, no rails. What are you doing now?"

"Playing Death March. What are you doing? I thought you were working."

"I am, a couple more hours. But I needed to ask you something. What was going through your head before you tried the gazelle thing?

"What do you mean? Nothing, really, except how to do it. You just go for it."

"I know that's not true. What was really going through your head before you tried it."

"Well, okay, sure, uh, there's always the broken neck and paralysis thing, but that's always, like, out there, so it's just WTF and you go."

"And you break your arm in two places and could have broken your neck and been paralyzed for the rest of your life for a skateboard trick."

"But I wasn't, and it wasn't just any trick. It was a 720 Gazelle Flip."

"No, you weren't, and it wasn't. You're right about that. Now get some rest after your video game fix. Tell your mom I love her. See you in a bit."

"Later, Dad."

What the fuck. Malcolm hits send.

CHAPTER CRIMINAL

I am not a crook.

So you see, students, journalism and truth have always had a very rocky marriage of mixed motives and ideals. There was a brief period, however, that we can call journalism's Golden Age, which spanned about thirty years in the last century. You can see how journalism worked in this so-called Golden Age, really its only Golden Age, by simply reading through the first Watergate story published under reporter Alfred E. Lewis's byline on Sunday, June 18, 1972. The most famous Watergate reporters, Bob Woodward and Carl Bernstein, were among eight reporters who contributed to the story, on a Saturday, back in the day when newsrooms were adequately staffed.

"What's so special about the Watergate story, Professor Ibid?"

What's that? Very quickly, then, Rob from Flagler Beach, I assumed everyone was familiar with this. The Watergate coverage – tracking the motives and players and machinations behind a bungled burglary of the Democratic Party's national headquarters – led to the resignation of President Richard Nixon, the only time a U.S. President has resigned from office. In other words, journalism did its job at the highest level, as a watchdog of authority and check against the abuse of power. It took more than two years of reporting to prove Nixon had knowledge of the crime, but the reporters never quit, and the newspaper, The Washington Post, had the resources to leave them on the story exclusively. The Golden Age was golden in advertising revenues and staffing too, not just the journalism it produced as a direct consequence.

So, if we can continue: Here is the top of that first story that is essentially an extremely well-done crime story, the cops beat on a Saturday, researched on the fly, in one day, by talented reporters and editors:

"Five men, one of whom said he is a former employee of the Central Intelligence Agency, were arrested at 2:30 a.m. yesterday in what authorities described as an elaborate plot to bug the offices of the Democratic National Committee here.

Three of the men were native-born Cubans and another was said to have trained Cuban exiles for guerrilla activity after the 1961 Bay of Pigs invasion.

They were surprised at gunpoint by three plain-clothes officers of the Metropolitan Police Department in a sixth floor office at the plush Watergate, 2600 Virginia Ave., NW, where the Democratic National Committee occupies the entire floor.

There was no immediate explanation as to why the five suspects would want to bug the Democratic National Committee offices or whether or not they were working for any other individuals or organizations.

A spokesman for the Democratic National Committee said records kept in those offices are "not of a sensitive variety" although there are "financial records and other such information."

Police said two ceiling panels in the office of Dorothy V. Bush, secretary of the Democratic Party, had been removed.

Her office is adjacent to the office of Democratic National

Chairman Lawrence F. O'Brien. Presumably, it would have been possible to slide a bugging device through the panels in that office to a place above the ceiling panels in O'Brien's office."

The story then goes into more detail on the men's backgrounds and affiliations, but as you can see from this top it offered only hints that there is more to the story, simply because the reporters and editors knew what questions to ask but did not have the answers yet. "There was no immediate explanation as to why..." and "...whether or not they were working for any other individuals..."

That's what the best journalism does: asks the right questions, then digs until the answers are discovered. The writing here offered no embellishment. These are stacked facts. It's not pretty, precision isn't pretty, but it's beautiful, and more powerful than any shouting into a radio or TV mic or tweet or thoughtext or headfeed will ever be. Black ink on paper. Look at the sequence of paragraphs, doing their job. Here's what we know, here's what we know, here's what we know, here's how we know it, here's what we don't know, here's what our sources say, here are more facts we've uncovered and verified. Giving the reader the news, assuring the reader of its legitimacy, its truth, its sourcing. Emotionless. Information. Verification. What news should be. What it was for about thirty years, from approximately the civil rights era through the Vietnam War through Nixon and up until Bill Clinton's first term, when it began to shift. Stacked facts became a less valuable currency over time, not enough to grab readers, viewers, listeners and eventually digital audiences, and the arrival of talk radio and Fux News in the

Nineties hastened the decline. The legitimate outlets had to somehow keep pace, so they tried to embrace the now-now-now look-at-me world of the internet and social media and stumbled badly. Real journalism, in other words, doesn't really know how to do biased, shouted, sound-byte, grandstanding journalism. And even though the heavyweights of print – New York Times, Washington Post, Wall Street Journal at the top of the list – along with a handful of digital outlets like Truth Network and Politico, found new inspiration with the scandal-plagued presidency of Donald Rump, a large part of his base – his cult – did not trust or believe them. Information and verification weren't enough. Truth became a worthless currency in the media landscape. Groupthink on the internet and social media became the cash cow, the most trusted source for news, one person on one device at a time reinforcing one hundred million others. And that's where we stand today. The truth you believe in your own little world is the only truth that matters.

CHAPTER PLAY

The Room Fell Silent With Unbearable Noise

A Play in One Act

The characters:

Trammell, a retired newspaper editor who now publishes a small-town newsletter called The Daily Truth that corrects lies appearing on local websites. His wife Karen died three years ago with Trammell's assistance and the help of her palliative care nurse. He lives alone with their deaf cat Norman in their house surrounded by their woods. Everything is still their. Trammell dislikes spending time with other humans, but as a favor to a former colleague he is working with a young reporter for the national Truth Network, covering the bombing of a cargo ship in Jacksonville, Florida earlier this morning. Two versions of the truth have come out so far, including an official 'ongoing investigation' type statement from President Cassandra Holland and a more widely shared statement from presidential challenger Daniel Hammerschmidt's camp alleging the bomber was a plant by the Democrats and may have involved Holland in an attempt to sway Tuesday's election. The man who posted the story implicating Holland minutes after the bombing is ...

The Colonel, a wealthy retired Army Captain who goes by The Colonel because his wife Li called him that, as in "You'll always be The Colonel to me" when he was denied a promotion, a fact he has never revealed nor lied about. He would tell the truth if asked. The Colonel got rich founding a cyber-security firm after twenty years of service in the Army's cyber command division at Ft. Irwin, California. He now runs a website called ironheel.com which promotes conservative causes from its headquarters in The Colonel's garage. Begun as a hobby shortly before Li's death, the website now serves as the primary national online outlet for TRIBE, the populist movement supporting Daniel Hammerschmidt for president. One TRIBE member The Colonel does not wish to see is... **Donnie Bone**, an unemployed roofer hooked on oxy, aka hillbilly heroin, and fentanyl who has been aligned with TRIBE for two years after a member visited his trailer park going door to door registering people to vote and promising jobs and help in cutting back on the pills, a plan that hasn't worked out for Donnie because TRIBE keeps dropping off pills that do the opposite, keep him hooked, unemployable and angry about being a forgotten American, the preferred state of the TRIBE voter. His membership has produced a couple of freelance jobs for Donnie, including arson on a fabric store owned by a Sikh man and most recently shooting two people (one survived) this morning. His payment for the latter was 'really good shit' provided to him, he was told, by The Colonel, who Donnie is now racing toward down Highway A1A with his dead overdosed girlfriend, **Baby**, bouncing like a dead person would bounce in the passenger seat. All of this obviously offstage until he gets here, although it might be interesting to show Donnie in frantic anger and haste driving the car, stage right behind the patio. The only eyewitness to the shootings, hiding among hibiscus bushes, was ... **Harold Dumas**, a computer sales rep and former IT manager at the Louisiana Superdome during Hurricane Katrina whose side endeavor to create a drone that could copy computer files through walls has inadvertently (but very much by design) made him a fugitive, accused of setting off a bomb on the hull of a cargo ship that killed four people inside and shooting two people (one, his wife Linda, survived) at his own home and now finds himself huddled in the woods next to the Jacksonville Beach library in a homeless camp. Sharing the secret space with Harold are his computer, his frantic mind directing frantic fingers on the keyboard, a one-eyed homeless woman he once knew, an alcoholic computer technician who knows a hacking secret that may clear Harold, and a young reporter named... **Lucy Neale**, an investigative reporter recently laid off by the Florida Times-Union in Jacksonville following the elimination of the investigative team in order to devote more resources to videos and social media. She has been hired by the Truth Network out of Washington D.C. to try to get to the bottom of this morning's bombing at the Port of Jacksonville, and is the only reporter to have tracked down Harold Dumas, through the savvy convergence of a library notice, a maintenance man and an old phone Dumas used decades ago. She is old school and digitally aware at once, using social media and the internet in service to the story but preferring face-to-face interviews over phone conversations whenever deadlines allow. Her demeanor and appearance suggest shyness but she is not shy. She is internal, third-person, skilled. Truth is what she discovers, knows and verifies. Truth is a very different animal for … **Dick Maestro**, a political power broker and president of TRIBE who felt relegated to the limited arena of Florida GOP politics until a chance encounter six years ago with a close-to-retirement Trammell helped propel him into the highest ranks of so-called 'dirty tricksters,' after he convinced major GOP players and donors on the national level to let him carry out a secret long-term plan to infiltrate TRIBE and rise in its ranks and save America from itself, a lofty end game he believed in his core although his core is just an external shell endlessly adaptable to any strategy breeding within, and whose love affair with his own cleverness would come back to bite him because of a comma, a goddamn comma.

The setting:

The expansive and expensive garage office of ironheel.com, overlooking the ocean in the small coastal city of Flagler Beach in northeast Florida. The stage is split to show both the inside of the garage as the primary scene and the oceanfront patio outside the garage's back door stage right. Two other settings-within-the-setting play critical roles — a Skype screen situated above the large central computer screen where ironheel.com's home page appears, and the front seat of an old beat up Corolla stage right behind the patio, barrelling toward it with Donnie driving frantically and Baby dead beside him.

Crashing waves can be heard faintly at all times. Fog drifts onto the patio and grows gradually thicker. The garage office matches The Colonel's military mindset, a clean and orderly setup upon a broad concrete floor, with one wall (facing the audience) covered in computer screens surrounding the main 10-feet-square homepage screen. A server sits in the corner with wire connections to all. The second wall (stage left) is lined with more servers, old-fashioned file cabinets and a massive oak desk and leather chair. The wall bordering the oceanfront patio (stage right) is merely a framework with a door and one window.

The Colonel sits at the desk, a compact man of 70 with close-cropped white hair and a thinning face of sharp angles, clean shaven. He wears an Army green T-shirt and khaki pants. Sitting near the desk in an office-style chair, out in the open, constantly stretching his back by bending forward, is Trammell, a baggy skinned but still muscled man of 72, with a dusting of hair on a nearly-bald head and a white Civil War-style goatee, bushy and unkempt.

Outside the garage, Donnie Bone, a ragged sinewy man of 27 with long wispy hair, is driving toward the home in the play's first half and arrives midway through the play. He carries his dead girlfriend, Baby, in his arms initially, pacing wildly on the patio behind the garage's back door, the Atlantic Ocean a few steps away with the crash of waves continual and a seagull's cry occasional. After several minutes of angry, inaudible mumbling, (not heard by the old slightly deaf men inside, who continue to talk as the play's primary dialogue), he lays Baby gently down as if she is sunbathing on the lounge chair beside the pool and stands over her, saying nothing.

The Colonel and Trammell are in the middle of a

conversation as the play opens. Trammell, introspective worn-out liberal misanthrope, leans forward on the folding chair and The Colonel, vital masculine conservative hiding loneliness, sits smartly at his desk, which holds a computer and neatly stacked manila files and nothing more.

COLONEL

(continuing a conversation begun before the play opens)

So you see, I do my blog every day but mostly I'm just a conduit. I'm the messenger. I aggregate other conservative news sites and even a couple of liberal ones, but we also have an agreement with TRIBE to break their official statements first on our national feed and on social media, and they pay us an annual fee. Ironically, that's what's giving me problems this morning. The TRIBE feed has locked me up. My home page is frozen with the statement as the lead item, and I can't figure out how to unfreeze it. It's a damn irritation. A major irritation. I need to get back to it.

TRAMMELL

(sitting up straight, rubbing his lower back)

I won't be long, Colonel. We're just trying to track the connection between TRIBE and today's bombing. Do you confirm what TRIBE sends you before you post it? This morning's, for instance?

COLONEL

I don't have the resources. I pretty much just rubber stamp it and post it. I've got two part-timers who handle local news — and get raked over the coals by you — but for national stuff, TRIBE is a reliable source. I trust them a lot more than I trust the lamestream liars. The odd thing about this morning is that I didn't seem to have a choice. The statement got posted by itself somehow and now I'm locked.

TRAMMELL

I will not argue the lamestream thing anymore. You win. The Washington Post and The New York Times and Truth Network are fake news. Part of a secret cabal of liberals out to take down the workin' man.

COLONEL

(smiling, then turning serious) Damn straight. But all we're really saying is that a free press doesn't mean biased press. And you smartass liberals in the media, to be honest, are the reason I went over to TRIBE. They stand for what I stand for and what I served for. A strong unvarnished America. Straightforward. One that doesn't bow down to anyone and believes in its people, the ones who made it what it is, not the ones who don't share our values. I know that sounds like the populist racist cliche but it's true. You're either with us or against us. TRIBE stands for the forgotten men and women of America and always will. They're the ones who built this country. They're this country's backbone.

TRAMMELL

(raising his head in a sign of life, speaking slowly, a tone of weary

rant)

Colonel, is it okay with you if I speak honestly, one old guy to another? This isn't a formal interview or anything, anyway.

COLONEL

Of course. Have at it. I really need to get back to repairing my website, but there's always time for a good argument with a liberal.

TRAMMELL

(smiling, then turning serious, the tone still a weary low-key rant)

That built-this-country line is total bullshit. I get so sick of it. Your forgotten folks built the bridges but it was other, smarter and more courageous people who built the laws that let people walk over them without being beaten and hosed. The great America is actually theirs. Hard work is not the highest measure of a life. Hard thought is. The only America the built-this-country crowd built is the racist, narrow-minded America being resurrected today. And they're forgotten people because they choose to be forgotten. They blame everyone else, but they had two options just like the rest of us: move forward in a changing world or die a slow death in the place and worldview you grew up in. Just because your daddy and your granddaddy worked in a parts plant doesn't mean you have to. Why do these guys limit themselves so? We don't have a caste system. We're not in Mumbai. We're not peasants in 18th century France. Everybody out there has the chance for a free K-through-12 education and then some kind of training after that. Daddies don't pull them out of third grade anymore to work in the fields. So just fucking do it. Change. Don't start working at the factory when you get out of high school. Read the fucking tea leaves. I was in an industry that was dying, and I learned what I had to to keep my job, hated it but learned it, but if I was starting out today I sure as hell wouldn't get into journalism — or the parts factory, in our other context — if I knew it was shrinking and dying. These forgotten shits actually just like to paint themselves as victims of the liberal elites, but they're actually digging their own graves. The world changes, you fucking change.

COLONEL

(clapping sarcastically)

Very fine speech from the profane liberal arts major looking down down down upon the working class masses. That's you, right, Trammell? I'll just take a stab: rich or at least well off parents, both college educated, suburban longhair, pot smoker, Led Zeppelin, car and college paid for by Daddy, right? Then as you got older, hated your hard-working parents, thought they were dumbshits because all they did was feed you and send you to college and give you the first down payment on a house.

TRAMMELL

Don't hate them. Hate what they stand for.

COLONEL

Whatever. An ingrate however you look at it. Every opportunity gift-wrapped for you and your response is to whine about how shitty the country is. I don't know what your mom and dad might say, but here's what the working men and women say: Fuck you. Not everyone is smart enough or has the money or opportunity to just throw away the life their family has known for generations and go in a completely different direction.

TRAMMELL

Then they're gonna get screwed every time, Colonel. Smart people move forward, dumb people stand still and then take it out on the rest of us by voting for a YouTube star.

COLONEL

There's a really destructive dumbness to liberals too, Trammell. It's called not being able to walk in another person's shoes, or in another person's brain. It's called thinking you're the only one who's right and everyone who disagrees is less than you.

TRAMMELL

Yeh, you're right. There's too much of that. I have it to a pretty strong degree. But it's got a backstory that somewhat covers my ass. I've been around blue collar guys and rural people all my adult life. Reporters get out and spend time with a lot of different people. Very few of them used to be hostile to me when I was younger. Some of them, the funny wise ones who became good sources, even got a little amusement out of me, the hippie college kid out mingling with the farmers and the roofers. But as I got older, things gradually and then quickly changed. I felt nothing but resentment when I entered a room. Something or someone — Rush Lamebaugh, Fux News, the NRA idiots, their own failure — turned them against everyone smarter than them. And over time the turn got harder, more intractable. And every other reporter who's been around for a while will tell you they've experienced the same thing. Until finally you just have to cover this group of people the best you can, professionally and fairly, because empathy is no longer possible. You can't empathize with someone who believes two plus two equals five and the media is lying when they say four. They've been hardwired by talk radio, by Fux, by ironheel.com.

COLONEL

We don't brainwash, for God's sake, Trammell. And maybe the resentment doesn't come from Rush or ironheel but from that weary whiny superior tone you guys always take, 24/7.

TRAMMELL

My wife used to tell me that. I don't mean to, and that's the truth. I'm just worn out, defeated, still having to talk about the same old primitive shit for seventy-two years now. The Dumb just keep multiplying. One of my great disappointments in life. That the smart guys don't win. Little victories here and there, but never the whole enchilada of humanity. It reached the point in my fifties where The Dumb began to taint everything. I couldn't listen to an intelligent news program without The Dumb infecting it. I meet a young person who seems bright and thoughtful and it brings sadness instead of hope. I know The Dumb will resent her and diminish her. I watch a good movie or listen to a smart, funny comedian, I know The Dumb will not understand it. We're going to be dead for a hundred years and they'll still be arguing about Adam and Eve. The weary part is the only one I feel anymore. It just comes out as whiny.

COLONEL

Most of what you say is demeaning horse shit, but I can relate to weary.

TRAMMELL

Yes, indeed. The common bond of all old Americans. But there's something at the heart of all this that I will never understand, Colonel. You're a smart guy, and I can't for the life of me understand why you'd be aligned with the Hammerschmidt crowd.

COLONEL

(A cat meows)

My cat is even getting sick of your bullshit, Trammell. And I'm not really a Hammer fan. I'm a conservative Republican who doesn't have a choice anymore. I wish we had a real old-school statesman on the ballot, but those guys are extinct or neutered.

TRAMMELL

(pause, looking around for a cat, continuing)

The reason is because The Dumb have become such a force. Statesmen don't appeal to them. Guys who smash things with a big hammer do. Can I rant some more?

COLONEL

Certainly. Takes my mind off the website. Haven't done this myself much since my wife and her friends used to argue with me.

TRAMMELL

Same here. Mine's gone too. We are two old widowers pissin' in the wind, comrade. This is kind of fun, though. Been a long time since I've ranted to anyone but my cat.

COLONEL

Mine's around here somewhere. Probably hiding from you.

TRAMMELL

You're probably right. New humans are frightening. Anyway, shall we keep ranting? This is going to sound like Hitler or Nietzsche or maybe George Wallace, take your pick, but this praise of the white working class and the white poor has been going on forever even though they are the ruin of this nation. Whitman called the common people the genius of the United States. How wrong is that. Writers love them for some reason I'll never understand, a search for authenticity, I guess. And there are some decent people among them, but they are as far from genius as you can get and shouldn't be deciding the future of the country. Democracy's fatal weakness, full participation by The Dumb. The old-school Republicans who want the oligarchy they used to have call it mob rule, and I'm kind of with them on that. I mean, go inside Tom

Joad's head and what's there? An uneducated dumbshit murderer who was given inspiring traits and honor and even a little journey into Emerson by the really smart writer who invented him. Ol' Tom would be voting for Hammerschmidt Tuesday, not Holland. Steinbeck, on the other hand, would vote for the capable, modern candidate. The smart people need to be the ones who decide, and the wise people who may not be book smart. Maybe there should be a logic test instead of a literacy test. Why are you voting for this person would be the only question.

COLONEL

I never knew elitists carried the same hate as racists. Your Tom Joad reference is so simplistic it sounds like one of my troll idiots. I did a thesis on "Grapes" back at West Point, a couple of hundred years ago. First of all, Steinbeck spent time with these folks and knew them, didn't just invent them. And Joad had every reason to be dragged down. He was exactly like those third graders who get pulled from school to work the farm, and then in the novel he brought some of it on himself for killing a man and going to prison, but the Depression and everything beyond his control in the Dust Bowl brought the weight crashing down too. And he tried to think things through —

TRAMMELL

Steinbeck thought for him.

COLONEL

— and bring some kind of honor to his life, but he just didn't have the knowledge to do it. I still remember the lines: I ain't thought it out all clear, Ma. I can't. I don't know enough.

TRAMMELL

Exactly. You're right, there's more to it. But that's kind of the point. Back then the working class poor had actual reasons to wail about the system. Now they don't. They bring it on themselves. The cycle of poverty ends when you pull yourself out of it. Keep going to high school. Don't get fucking pregnant at fifteen. Go to trade school. Run away from it if you have to. Do something different for God's sake than what your parents and cousins and granddads did. What they did isn't working. Nothing to lose. And the simple phrase 'I don't know enough' should maybe disqualify them from voting.

COLONEL

And then Democrats would lose about half of their minority voters, too. Or are they okay with you?

TRAMMELL

There's a difference. If you are uneducated but wise, you can vote. If you know what's right and decent, you can vote. Same holds true for rural white voters, black voters, Hispanic voters, rich white voters. We need to figure out a way to distinguish who is wise enough, aware enough, decent enough, to cast a logic-based honorable vote. The land-owning white male gentry was a little too narrow.

COLONEL

That's the most ridiculous thing I've ever heard. The silver spoon Zeppelin pothead decides who votes. Everyone deserves a vote. It's the candidate's job to inspire them.

TRAMMELL

With fucking YouTube videos and wacko Russian social media bullshit?

COLONEL

Well, you're right. We should probably do a bit better than that. But that doesn't mean a Harvard law professor should be the president every four years. We just need to get back to decent, conservative men or women who care about their country and care about the people who love their country and who lead our entire nation, not lord it over everyone else like the Democrats. They're just like you, Trammell. You live inside your head too much. You intellectualize everything. Sometimes you need to just push ahead and do what's needed, what's required. You'd never make it in the Army –

TRAMMELL

No I would not.

COLONEL

— because A) you interrupt, and B) because you'd have to look at all sides of an order and decide whether or not carrying out the order was in the best interest of success or failure or The Big Picture or the philosophical underpinning of the war. Can't do that shit. You weigh the immediate risks, argue your point quickly with your superior officer if you disagree and then defer to his judgment and carry out the fucking order. You're not Rodin's Thinker. You do your job. And I've learned all this about you after spending fifteen minutes with you. I've known plenty of your type, a lot of my wife's former friends. Your approach to politics and life is the same. Endless analysis, endless debate, looking down your noses at the ones who actually live life and love their children and just want to move forward themselves with a little house or double-wide. And that means sometimes you vote for a guy that you want to have a beer with, and there's nothing wrong with that. You pick your leader, I'll pick mine.

TRAMMELL

Except that drinking beer and being your buddy are not qualifications for the job.

COLONEL

Doesn't matter what you think. To the guy who voted for him, they are.

(A Maine Coon cat walks out from under The Colonel's desk. The argumentative old men shift quickly to a conversational calm.)

TRAMMELL

What a beautiful Maine Coon.

COLONEL

There you are, big man. I'm just out here talking to an uppity liberal whose brain isn't quite right. That's Stephen. Stephen King lived in Maine, so, Stephen.

(Stephen the cat stops to scratch himself.)

TRAMMELL

Fleas have been getting worse. Do you flea comb him?

COLONEL

Nope. Use one of the back of the neck things. Must be wearing off. They don't really work very well sometimes now that we're hot most of the year.

TRAMMELL

You're missing a real treat, then, Colonel. A little fun cruelty in your day. Have you ever watched a flea drown? You should use a flea comb on Stephen for no other reason than to drop the little bastards in water and watch them drown. They herk and jerk and even try to jump inside the water, and sometimes get little air bubbles on their tiny mouths. They crawl up the side of the bowl, weighed down but still alive. You have to poke them back in. They fight with every ounce of energy they can muster. And they do this — sometimes for five seconds or more if the air bubble forms — even though they are utterly worthless creatures who serve no purpose except to gorge on their own desire, reproduce and spread death and destruction and annoyance. It's incredible that even the worthless put up a fight. Why don't they just go ahead and drown? The will to survive never leaves, until it does, eh?

(a loud angry voice can be heard shouting "Colonel!" from offstage, and Donnie Bone turns away from Baby on the lounge chair and walks closer to the house on the back patio.)

DONNIE BONE

Colonel! Colonel! Are you in there, motherfucker? Get your motherfucking ass out here, Colonel!

(Both Trammell and The Colonel are startled nearly out of their seats.)

COLONEL

(in a low voice) What the hell...

TRAMMELL

(whispering) Guy sounds high on PCP or something. How'd he get on your back patio?

COLONEL

You can just walk up the beach from the public park about a hundred yards south. I've had plenty of pillheads and meth-heads and black gangbangers come up here. The cameras and the alarm usually scare them off. I don't know who the fuck this guy is who knows my name somehow, though.

(The Colonel pulls his gun from the desk, walks to the door and shouts through it. Trammell stays put in his chair, leaning forward. Donnie paces slowly but wildly like an addict gone far beyond strung out.)

COLONEL

Who are you and what do you want? I have a Glock pointed at you through the door as we speak.

DONNIE

Go ahead and shoot me, asshole! I do not fucking care at this point. I'm the guy you tried to kill with poisoned shit, man. I shot two people for you and your asshole friends and you kill my Baby as fucking thanks. Get your ass out here and tell me what's going on.

COLONEL

I'll do no such thing. I don't know what you're talking about. I'm calling the cops if you don't leave now.

DONNIE

Go ahead and call them! I'll tell them the truth. That you hired me as a hit man and then tried to kill me!

(The Colonel glances back at Trammell with scared but resolute eyes, then keeps talking through the door.)

COLONEL

Who told you that? Where are you getting this wild story?

DONNIE

You told me, motherfucker. I've got your texts from starting in, like, August.

COLONEL

I never sent you any texts. I don't even know you.

DONNIE

(pulling his phone from his pocket) Is your phone number 386-555-5385?

COLONEL

Yes, how did you –

DONNIE

Then you are lying through your teeth, motherfucker, and I've got the proof right here in my hand. You rich TRIBE shits are just like rich shits everywhere. Now get your ass out here!

(Suddenly the window pane of the door shatters and Donnie's fist bursts through, bloodied and splintered with shards grabbing for the door handle. The Colonel turns and lunges toward the door with gun drawn.)

COLONEL

Back away, you little son-of-a-bitch! Back away or I'll kill you! You will never get through this door!

(Donnie backs away and quite suddenly recoils into himself, holding his bloodied hand. The pain shocks him into helplessness.

His voice loses its fury.)

DONNIE

Damn you goddam you fucking damn you. You think you're so fucking great in your fucking mansion. You think someone like me is a piece of shit, some motherfucker, some....Forget it, man. Fucking forget it.

(Donnie fades to a mumble and he slumps, as if his muscles cannot hold him up, cradling his phone and his life, then suddenly turns toward Baby, thinking he heard her say something, and walks over to her and strokes her hair, tells her shhh, shhh, it will be alright. He calms, his entire body, his entire being, calms, and he sits on the end of the lounger, resting his hand on Baby's leg.)

DONNIE

We're in a shitload of trouble, Baby, but I'm trying to get us out of it and it's not so bad when you think about it, not a bad way maybe. Look where we are. We're at a mansion on the ocean, and we're rich as shit and sittin' out by our pool, looking at the ocean. It's foggy and you can't see it much but it's still the most beautiful thing you've ever seen, Baby. The fog makes it even more beautiful maybe 'cause you know it's there. *(Pauses, thinking about what to say to her, how to say it.)* We're never going to get any better than this. I'm really sorry, Baby. Samantha. I never call you Sam anymore. If I hadn't hurt my fucking back none of this would have happened. The fucking doc just kept giving me pills and giving me pills and didn't give a shit about me at all. It's his fucking fault, really. No no no. It's my fucking fault. My brother went up to Georgia and found work. I could've done the same fucking thing. He fucking set his mind to it and got trained as a machinist. What the fuck did I do. Took some scam class for fast talkers on those radio ads, the fine print at the end you can never understand. Remember when I practiced, Baby? Individual-results-may-vary-Offer-not-valid-in-Rhode-Island. Remember? I got pretty good, but then where the fuck do you work? They didn't tell you that. Fuckers. So I just kept gettin' high, and brought you with me down that sorry fucking road. We coulda started that little tomato farm if I hadn't been so fucked up. If I hadn't been such a stupid shit motherfucker. That's what my dad called me, and he was fucking right. I'm sorry, Baby. I'm really sorry. And I'm really tired. I don't think I've ever been this tired. The ocean's calm, Baby. You can barely see it but you can tell it's calm. What do you think, Baby? I don't think it's ever gonna be better than this. Sitting by a pool overlooking the ocean, and the ocean is calm. I feel calm. I feel real calm and real strong.

Calm strong, like those SEALS who knew they might die on TV the other night. That's how I feel, Baby, fucking calm strong.

(Donnie stands and bends over to pick Baby up and with her in his arms he walks toward the ocean, talking to her looking straight ahead.)

DONNIE

Calm strong, Baby. We are calm strong. Just like the fucking SEALS on that show the other night.

(Stage right, Donnie stops still holding Baby nearly vanished into the fog, remaining only as blurred impressionism. Donnie begins a low, extended wail, almost a battle cry, almost angelic, as if the fog had voice. Inside, The Colonel and Trammell are still listening, heads poised at angles. The Colonel walks over holding his gun and looks out the window, sees Donnie standing holding Baby in the deeper fog at the edge of his patio. At that moment, a SKYPE screen high on the wall above the main screen blinks and crackles on, scaring both of them. Fog drifts into the room through the shattered door glass. Lucy and Harold are leaning into the Skype screen in a wooded setting.)

LUCY

Trammell! Trammell! Are you there? We're at a homeless camp in Jax Beach and I need to talk to you right away. Some amazing stuff to tell you.

TRAMMELL

(steps out into the Skype screen's view)

Lucy, I'm here. The Colonel is here, too. Is that Harold Dumas with you?

HAROLD

Yes, it's me. I'm in hiding, or thought I was, and Lucy found me. But I'm glad she did. I think with the help of our friends here and a couple of others Lucy uncovered we have enough to clear me and—

(In the middle of Harold's sentence, there are repeated clicking sounds and the dull diminishing buzz of computers and screens ramping down. The wall with its huge screen and all of its smaller screens surrounding the main screen goes gradually quickly dark and the Skype transmission operating on its separate signal locks up with Lucy and Harold frozen in mid-excitement. The room suddenly has no computer presence or digital life beyond the frozen Skype image of Lucy and Harold in the homeless camp. The two old men sit in dim natural light coming from the windows as more fog drifts in through the shattered door. Donnie Bone's wail outside interrupts one minute of silence. Then the huge screen slowly revives, and into view from pixelated to focused to monstrous emerges the Aryan jaw and face and precisely parted silver hair of Dick Maestro. He smiles down at The Colonel.)

MAESTRO

Hello, Colonel. It's been a long time.

(The colonel pauses, shakes disbelief from his head, looks up at the big screen.)

COLONEL

I've never met you. Are you Dick Maestro? And why are you on my main screen? How are you on my main screen? I didn't send you there. You must be the one who fixed the TRIBE statement on my carousel. And now you've taken over the whole site? What the hell are you doing to me, Maestro?

MAESTRO

A better question would be what have you done to yourself, Colonel.

COLONEL

I have no idea what you're talking about. You're the second person today making absolutely no sense.

MAESTRO

You don't lie very well, Colonel.

COLONEL

I can't lie about what I don't know.

(Donnie wails outside on the patio.)

MAESTRO

What's that wailing, Colonel? Sounds like an animal in a trap.

COLONEL

Never mind that, shithead. You probably already know.

(Maestro smiles just barely at the corners of his mouth.)

Tell me what the fuck you're doing and what it has to do with me.

MAESTRO

The world was laughing at us, Colonel. You realized that, of course. You were never part of the TRIBE riff-raff anyway, were you? Like our sad friend outside was. The oxy-heroin-fentanyl crowd. The laid off factory workers. The millions of people who can't cut it in the modern world and like to blame smart people for their own shortcomings. We always thought that was a good thing, didn't we? Whatever you want to say about it, resentment works to rally the people. Get out the vote, you know. Killing unborn babies or immigrant invasion, whatever opium the people need, right, Colonel? But the truth is you need people who can think at least a little. And if they can't, well, you just need to do their thinking for them.

COLONEL

What are you getting at, Maestro? You're not making a point so much as insulting the very people who get your guys elected and pay your salary.

MAESTRO

Oh, they never paid my salary, Colonel. But that's off point. Back to the matter at hand. I never know quite how to read you retired military guys. Never served myself. Doesn't pay enough. If you're asking me to kill someone or be killed, you sure as hell better pay me something, right?

COLONEL

That's off point even more and you're a cowardly bastard for saying it.

MAESTRO

Right. Right. You officers are the biggest mystery. Intelligent and bullheaded. Meticulous and ludicrous. All at once. You're either building ships in bottles or plotting to take over Washington. You obviously chose the latter.

COLONEL

Again, motherfucker. What the hell are you talking about?

MAESTRO

The bomb at the port. Four people dead. Setting it off and then blaming it on Harold Dumas. Calling him a plant of the Dems, trying to hang it on President Holland. I must say I admire your ambition. Your chutzpah, to borrow from our Jewish friends.

COLONEL

I did nothing of the sort, sir.

MAESTRO

I'm sure you said that a lot during your time in the service, Colonel. Especially when you got disciplined for that rogue drone software you created at Fort Irwin.

COLONEL

What software? That's an outright lie, you son-of-a-bitch! A total fabrication! I never created a rogue drone and I was never disciplined once!

MAESTRO

Your Army records indicate otherwise, Colonel. Kind of explains the drone bomb specs on your computer. And those texts you sent to our mutual friend Donnie Bone are pretty damning, too. Oh, and there's the DNA match on the trumpet flower that killed his girlfriend to the bush in your front yard. Beautiful but deadly. That was Li's landscaping idea, wasn't it? Of course the real victim in all this is poor Mr. Dumas, who's in hiding somewhere, a library maybe? A homeless camp? On a screen just above me? And whose wife Linda is hanging on by a thread. Hope she makes it. She can corroborate Mr. Bone's involvement and the files that you and your Ukrainian partners stole from Harold's computer. Never could quite get your own rogue drone to work, could you, Colonel? And then of course, the texts to Mr. Wagner, rest his soul. Oh, and please don't think this conversation will be of any help to you. I see you trying to record it. It is strictly a courtesy call. I have revealed nothing here but your guilt.

COLONEL

What's to stop me from going in and deleting permanently all this shit you planted, or just blowing up my entire system right now?

MAESTRO

Well, it has all been copied and transferred to the appropriate federal, state and local agencies, so feel free. The so-called planted shit you mention isn't planted at all, and investigators will see that too when they do their forensics. It's like the poison the Russians like to use. You can't see something that can't be seen.

(Realizations click like subterranean panic inside The Colonel's

brain. His body remains tall and proud with a slowly evolving sunkenness.)

COLONEL

You fucking bastard. I am innocent and I will prove it and I will be cleared.

MAESTRO

Good luck with that, Colonel. I have a different perspective on this, anyway. I see you as a hero of sorts in your guilt. Pity about the four men who died, but the time was right for some kind of dramatic change, a catalyst. We were sliding into a cesspool of mob rule, Colonel. The American juggernaut became a joke. We lost standing. We lost influence. No one believed or respected the clown. Only clowns that kill are respected. Look at the most brutal despots in world history, Colonel. I know you're a student of history. They have all been evil clowns. Satans at the circus. Caligula. Hitler. Amin. Jung Un. Mao. Stalin. Silly little sociopaths who put strangleholds on entire nations. Spoiled little chubbies who will poison or behead you if they don't get their way. Our little chubbie wanted to join their club but America wouldn't let him in. So he just made us into a joke instead. And when we are a joke, Colonel, the opinions and influence of wealthy, powerful men are diminished. They were, in fact, almost eliminated. Those opinions matter, Colonel. Their wealth matters. Their power matters. Justice and order is nothing but the advantage and benevolence of the strong. We must, for our very survival, get back to the old ways. Restore a legitimate conservative party. What we like to call as a joke the WOW party. Well-off whites. They've lost their way, ready to Bring Down the Hammer on Tuesday, for God's sake. We need them back. A liberal senator once described our mission disparagingly as a modern-day law of the jungle: Me rich. You not. Status quo good. Mob rule bad. There's a lot of truth to that, actually, and it produces a stable, prosperous nation that's very liquid. And even those you might not expect, the men who control information, who have always presented themselves as liberal giants, now see the light. If this ridiculous scheme of yours can shatter faith in the TRIBE narrative, and maybe, just maybe, this is the one that can finally do it, then we can shift the poor forgotten dumbshits back into Forgottenland where they belong. We don't need any more clowns. The actor was good for us back in the last century, kept the WOW faction happy and solidified the South, but the first true clown really caught us by surprise, brought in a huge group of idiots who fell for his bullshit. Most of them had never even voted before. The clown made us pathetic and I really don't like being pathetic. And then it somehow got worse. A roller coaster of backlash presidencies – nationalist clown, progressive celebrity, nationalist clown, and on and on the democracy joke goes.

Colonel, God bless you, we're just hoping your little charade turns things around, gives Hammerschmidt enough of a blow. He can't win on early ballots alone. And you should also know, Colonel, I've talked with President Holland about this, and we are about to hold a joint press conference. I'm sure you'll want to be watching, so I'll put it up on your homepage. We're not taking any chances. A new little tidbit of news will be coming your way, too. The final dagger, shall we say. And I see your friend Mr. Trammell taking notes in his little notebook and trying to record it with his little cassette recorder. Haven't seen one of those in years. But it won't matter. As I've noted, this has been strictly a courtesy call. I've already left the TRIBE base far behind, so my disregard for them can't hurt me. And I believe my willingness to fully cooperate with investigators will become apparent soon. So in truth, the only thing I have revealed in this conversation, as I mentioned before, is your guilt.

And Mr. Trammell, one last thing. That final dagger I mentioned? You deserve credit for that. You are in truth the man who saved America. In fact, I could ring you up as an accessory if I chose to, so don't think that recorder or your little notebook filled with little notes is going to help.

TRAMMELL

I'm just here for the story, Maestro. What the fuck are you talking about?

MAESTRO

You, Mr. Trammell. I'm talking about you. Saving America. Through me. We are not so very far apart in our thinking.

TRAMMELL

You're still not making any sense.

MAESTRO

Back in the day, Mr. Trammell. You were an editor at the Daytona Beach News-Journal. Retiring the next month, as I recall. I was state chairman of the Republican Party. I was mainstream GOP back then. Always have been, really. I appeared before your editorial board. We were just starting to get overrun on a state level by the clowns who stole our party, and after the meeting we were out smoking and you joked about how to get our party back. Cut off the head, so to speak, when Hammerschmidt was first making noises about running. Do you recall?

TRAMMELL

I do not. I vaguely remember the meeting, maybe, but nothing about a conversation or saving America.

MAESTRO

I'm the one saving it, but I'll give you credit for the idea. This is what you said, Mr. Trammell. I wrote it down while we were standing there. Exact words or almost: There's only way to get rid of this guy, and that's to go even lower than anyone imagined. Murder won't do it. His cult won't believe it. The old 'shoot someone on Fifth Avenue' thing all over again. He's got his cult convinced that law enforcement and judges are part of some deep state conspiracy out to get their man and honest, hard-working

Americans. Only one thing will do it. Hit the angry white male where it hurts, right in the balls, where their brain is. First, you've got to show that their hero has a freakishly small dick, and second, you've got to show him fucking little boys.

Do you remember now, Mr. Trammell? You were refreshingly blunt with your solution.

TRAMMELL

(pause, small laugh)

Yep. I guess I do remember that. It was just a joke. In poor taste. I was pretty worn out by life at that point. And that turns you into a bastard telling bad jokes.

MAESTRO

A joke from a liberal bastard that actually made sense, however. And do you recall my response? I upped the ante on your idea. Money. You have to get money to them somehow, or they'll just shift from the baby fucker to some other bozo. We need to shut them up for good with a little cash. That was my contribution to your plan. And in the car a few weeks later, I heard an old song that just made me feel good, and made me tap my fingers on the steering wheel, and I just couldn't stop. That's when it really started all coming together. And so, you see, Mr. Trammell, the story began with you. I shifted from the GOP over to TRIBE the next year, and the rest, shall we say, is the future. So thank you, Mr. Trammell, for propelling our nation to a new era, same as the old era but the beards have all grown longer overnight. The Who, wasn't it? Everything will be right again. Old money will return, new money will rise, democracy will be saved. So, shall we get right to it? And oh, good day and thank you for your service, Colonel. Or should I say Captain. And one last thing, the FBI and your local Sheriff's Office will be arriving shortly.

(Silence. Trammell taking notes in slightly stunned fashion. Colonel staring at screen, where the transmission has ended but Maestro's face, locked digitally, looks down in monstrous benevolence. The frozen Skype image of Lucy and Harold remains. The silence continues for nearly a minute, interrupted twice by Donnie Bone wailing. The Colonel begins to pace, his posture still resolute.)

COLONEL

I believed in their mission. I'm so sorry, Li. You were right. I never needed the racist shit, or the YouTube idiot, or Maestro. I worked with a lot of these guys, and a lot of these women, back in training, and in the company. Hired them. Loved them. They came from TRIBE families before there was TRIBE. Nineteen year olds who had nothing in front of them, no future, and came to me to learn. They were good kids, and they believed in America, and a lot of them became first-rate programmers and analysts. But mostly they loved their country. That's what I just don't see anymore. That's why I helped TRIBE. The only reason. I believe in America. I don't see a future. I'm strong enough to go through all this shit but I won't. It dishonors me. It dishonors Li. It dishonors our time on Earth.

TRAMMELL

You're a soldier, Colonel. This is your new mission.

(The Colonel stops pacing. Looks out the broken window brimming in fog.)

COLONEL

Yes, a new mission. You're right. This is my new mission. For me and for Li. I can run out there and try to get this stupid kid's phone. You tell them that, Trammell. Hacks are easier to decipher in a phone than they would be in my system. I ran out there to try and get this kid's phone and try to save him. I can prove those texts that ordered the hit were from somewhere else and not from me. That's what I'll do. If anything goes wrong, tell them that, Trammell.

DONNIE

(whispering out on the patio)

I love you, Baby. I'll always love you. Here we go. We're going in now. We can do this, Baby. Calm strong. Calm strong, Baby.

(Donnie walks carrying Baby into the fog and the ocean beyond until he disappears. The Colonel walks to the door and looks through the broken glass. No one is there except fog. He opens the door and walks outside himself.)

COLONEL

(speaking in a monotone) I need to get his phone. You are absolutely right. I have a new mission. I can figure out the hack if I

can get his phone. Tell them I tried to save him and get his phone. Tell them I tried to save him.

(The Colonel marches like a soldier into the fog and the ocean beyond until he disappears.)

TRAMMELL

(He runs to the broken window, shouting into the fog)

Colonel! Colonel! We'll figure this out! You're an old man, Colonel! You'll never drag him in! Colonel! Colonel!

(Trammell stares into the fog, hand over his mouth and beard. In a low voice...)

And you have no intention of dragging him in, do you.

(Trammell turns and walks slowly back to the center of the room. He picks up his cellphone to call someone but shakes his head What's the use? The cops are on their way. The Skype screen crackles to life. Harold's voice interrupts Trammell's silent reverie for the Colonel.)

HAROLD

Colonel, are we back up? Colonel, don't do anything with the files that Maestro planted in your system.

TRAMMELL

The Colonel's not here anymore, Harold. Is Lucy still with you?

LUCY

I'm here, Trammell. Where's The Colonel? We have what we think is some good news for him. We've been kicking ass.

TRAMMELL

I don't know where he is. Foreverland. With his wife. I don't know. I couldn't stop him. I couldn't do anything. I'm too old. He ran out just now but it's already too late. I couldn't save him. He died a heroic death, trying to clear himself from all this shit. He ran out into the ocean to try and save the wailing kid — the guy who apparently tried to murder your wife, Harold — from drowning himself so he could get his phone. He thought he could break the hacker's code or something on the phone.

HAROLD

He didn't even have to do that at all. Shit. I can save him. Can't you get out there and try to get him back to the shore? Between me and Lucy and this other Harold I met here, we may have enough to put it all on Maestro.

TRAMMELL

Too late. Too late. I can't save anyone. The Colonel is gone. Into the fog. I'm sorry. Very sorry. *(long pause)* What do you and Lucy have?

HAROLD

I can't believe he killed himself before I could get to him. He's a military guy, for God's sake.

LUCY

That explains a lot. Lost honor. The worst thing that could happen.

TRAMMELL

He didn't kill himself. He tried to save the kid. Remember that. He died trying to save the kid and get the phone.

HAROLD

But it was fucking five minutes or less that I missed him.

TRAMMELL

I can't save him, Harold. It's over. I'm helpless in this. Like a run-over raccoon still alive.

HAROLD

I don't know what you're talking about, Trammell, but I can't believe you're not even trying when we can nail Maestro and clear The Colonel at the same time. You really must be old and worn out, man.

TRAMMELL

It's not that. Or at least not all that. I'm just not willing to die for The Colonel. I would go out there in a heartbeat if it was Karen. Or you, Lucy. Someone more valuable, or not that. That's not right. The Colonel is valuable. But he's also ready. Ready to see Li again. I'm not interfering with that.

HAROLD

Whatever. We've got to move on this anyway. I need copies of his main programs. You'll have to figure it out, Trammell, before the cops come. I'll walk you through it. There's a homeless guy here, believe it or not, who knew about a RAT that is virtually undetectable, but you can find it if you go through one specific backdoor. It uses a comma code, one fucking comma, to get to your files. There are no commas in code, of course, but this one disguises itself as a slash so you don't see it. But your computer does, and attacks it like a virus, creating short-term backup files while it weeds out the virus. The hackers snatch up the backups in the 60 seconds they exist, alter them, and use the same process to replace the originals in your system with you none the wiser. I think I can prove this, on my system and The Colonel's. And if we had the crazy pillhead's phone who shot my wife, I think we could prove it on those texts, too. This homeless guy was a miracle worker. I might give him a job when all of this is over. If it's ever over.

LUCY

We don't need his phone. Trammell, James has an insider in Maestro's office, calls himself Inconsequential Man, who sent him Maestro's personal phone records going back more than a year. For a guy who essentially runs the world, he was dumb as a rock for trusting this aide. He had all his office phones encrypted and secured but his personal phones just had basic security. They were burner phones and he bought new ones every two weeks, but the aide copied the records every Friday night. He even recorded the conversations. Played Maestro bigtime. James says the aide was a diehard TRIBE guy but hated Maestro to the core, thought he was a fake. Anyway, the records show Maestro called virtually everyone connected to this. He talked with Wagner, the guy who was killed. He talked with Donnie Bone, the kid who did the killing. Bone called him, from Harold's house, after the shooting this morning, but the number he called was The Colonel's. That's another amazing source we got. Some guy who works for Impetus surveillance – he didn't give me his name, so we'll have to verify time stamps and such – sent me audio and video from Harold's house this morning. It's incredible, Trammell. Maestro – I assume it's Maestro — doesn't say anything into the phone except, "This is not the colonel. Do not call again," but the surveillance guy locked in the real number, and I know a cop who does voice analysis. So I think we have Maestro on the hit job, Trammell. But here's something weird that has me a little worried. When he sent the file, the surveillance guy just said in the text, Here's a never-tried-before trick. What do you think that means?

TRAMMELL

I have no idea. I hope it doesn't mean he altered it.

LUCY

James has already sent the file to his hacker friend. We'll make sure.

TRAMMELL

You really are kicking ass, Miss Lucy.

LUCY

That's not all, Trammell. The phone records show that Maestro called the CEOs for the five largest information companies in the last year, promising them 'huge returns' on some kind of investment that would put more eyes on their ads than ever before and target them more precisely than ever before. I'm not sure where or if those guys fit into all this, and I'm not sure either about the Crotch family heirs and the Vegas billionaire's widow, but we have calls from Maestro to them in the phone records too. Haven't had time to listen to all of it.

TRAMMELL

Man. Nice work. You'll have to tell the investigators. Make copies and break the story first.

HAROLD

Get me a contact at the FBI. Tell them I'll be in touch. Lucy can work with the local sheriff's office down there. I'm not coming out of hiding yet with all this shit flying around. Lucy's still got some loose ends to tie up before she updates her story, too. Now go over to The Colonel's main computer on his desk and I'll tell you how to send his files to me. I'm going to link in from here and I'll do most of the heavy lifting. You'll just have to hit a couple of buttons on the keyboard. We should be able to work around the control matrix Maestro's guys installed. Shouldn't take too long.

TRAMMELL

You don't know who you're dealing with here, Harold. I used a cassette recorder and a notebook today. Nobody hacks notebooks.

(Harold laughs and starts inputting code into his computer)

LUCY

Hey, Trammell. Forgot to tell you. Your tip on Southern Poverty paid off, too. Your Smithson guy isn't there anymore, but another IT guy checked on it and said the name Harold Dumas just suddenly appeared on the cyber-terrorist list and then came off just as quickly, and The Colonel's real name, Frederick Branch, I think it was, replaced it. No one on the staff did it. So we have that, too. They're trying to trace the hack. And on another note, isn't it amazing that a comma could possibly bring down one of the most powerful men in Washington?

TRAMMELL

Yes, it is, Lucy, and thank you for noticing. Punctuation wins the day.

HAROLD

There's really no time to be laughing, people. Let's move on this. Trammell, when you see my message pop up on The Colonel's screen, just hit control-enter to get inside his program, then when another box pops up, just hit OK, and the upload will start.

(Trammell goes through the two steps.)

TRAMMELL

Done. Is it working on your end?

HAROLD

Yep. They're on the way. Now all we have to do is wait and we'll have everything –

(A voice sounds loudly from the main screen, interrupting Harold. An image of Dick Maestro standing at a podium on the White House south lawn appears, with President Cassandra Holland behind his left shoulder.)

MAESTRO

Thank you, President Holland. Hello, fellow Americans. My name is Dick Maestro and I am the president of TRIBE. I have always believed in our cause, our mission, our values, but

I am here today to tell you that I am a liar, and everything TRIBE stands for is a lie, and everything Daniel Hammerschmidt stands for is a lie.

This is very difficult for me and will likely either send me to prison or ruin my career or both, but with the death of four American workers in today's bombing at the Port of Jacksonville, I can be silent no longer. The statement I issued this morning suggesting the involvement of President Holland and the Democratic National Committee in this horrific act was false. Let me be clear. It was fake news. I was the one who wrote the statement and I am coming clean because I cannot be a party to murder. This bombing was murder, and TRIBE was behind it and Daniel Hammerschmidt was behind it.

Yes, the man who wants to be your president murdered four men today, good and decent men, hard working Americans, men who were probably going to vote for him. There was no bomber planted by the Democrats, no scheme by President Holland to undermine Hammerschmidt's campaign. In truth it was just the opposite. This was engineered and carried out by TRIBE.

Let me be clear: TRIBE murdered four men to try and win an election. President Holland had nothing to do with it. She is completely innocent, and just as horrified as I am. One of our chapter presidents in Florida and another member who operates the TRIBE-sponsored website ironheel.com concocted this plan to shatter President Holland's re-election campaign four days before the vote and put Daniel Hammerschmidt in a stronger position to win. Now four men are dead. This was fake news, a scheme, a deadly scheme, complete with falsified records and invented documents, and I was an accomplice in it until this morning. No more. No one was supposed to die.

Let me make myself clear. The fake news on this did not come from the mainstream media. It came from us, from TRIBE, from ironheel, from Breitfart, from Fux, from all of us on this end. We are the fake news and have always been the fake news. I know that better than anyone because I was on the inside. No more. For all you TRIBE members out there, hear me out: You have been duped. If you can't bring yourself to vote for Mrs. Holland this Tuesday, then go third party or just stay away from the polls. Do not vote for Hammerschmidt. He is a murderer. We can't live on lies anymore. I can't live a lie anymore.

I hereby publicly resign my position with TRIBE effectively

immediately. I know the great Americans who are members of TRIBE will despise me, but I hope they will believe me on this as well. TRIBE and Daniel Hammerschmidt are feeding you lies, they are murderers, and I'm leaving them regardless of consequences. I hope to devote myself to my family and to working toward the search for a viable and truthful Republican conservative to support in the next presidential election. I have already given investigators full access to TRIBE's computers and will continue to give them my full cooperation. If I am charged and convicted with a crime I will of course serve my time. But it will have been worth it. Thank you, President Holland, and thank you, America. I apologize deeply and completely for my role in this.

(Maestro vanishes gradually from screen, a slow fade to black that transitions his head, then face, to ghostly disembodiment then fades to only eyes for several seconds then total black. Immediately the ironheel.com website resumes transmission and a beautiful female android with attractive cleavage dominates the screen delivering breaking news)

"A lawsuit filed Friday by the families of five boys under the age of 10 alleges that presidential frontrunner Daniel Hammerschmidt sexually abused the boys earlier this year during a summer camp for Mixed Martial Arts fans at Hammerschmidt's New Jersey mansion.

"The families allege that Hammerschmidt gave the boys gifts ranging from virtual life helmets to skateboards in exchange for oral sex and anal intercourse.

"The suit also alleges that Hammerschmidt struck two of the boys in the face and forced them to eat their own feces when he caught them making disparaging remarks to each other about the size of his penis. Hammerschmidt has faced rumors in the past from three of his ex-wives that his genitalia had shrunk due to long-term steroid use.

"A spokesman for the Hammerschmidt campaign vehemently denied the lawsuit's allegations and referred a reporter to the candidate's Thoughtext account. Here is the first cloudburst from Hammerschmidt, posted on Thoughtext about 30 seconds ago: @REALHAMMER – Total FAKE LAWSUIT. Kids lying. Where is smocking gun? Families paid millions by Dems to hand election to low-IQ ape in heels. WON'T WORK. I'M WINNING. NO PROBLEMS DOWN THERE! Ask any woman, I fuck like a hung rabbit. I am role model and hero for boys. Total BULLSHIT. Black WHORE in White House will do anything! BRING DOWN THE HAMMER!!

(The Hammerschmidt thoughtext remains on the main screen below the buxom news reader, and smaller cloudbursts from other Thoughtext accounts quickly begin appearing all around it across the entire wall of The Colonel's garage, popping up for 10 seconds brightly, then receding to low-level light – still legible – as another appears brightly elsewhere, each remaining long enough for the theater audience to read and never be left without a new cloudburst, again and again and again and again as the wall becomes covered with Thoughtexts.)

HAMMER STILL GETS MY VOTE!!! No boys, no bomb, no black bitch!! Take Racial Identity Back Evermore!! TRIBE RULES!! BRING DOWN THE HAMMER!!

Maestro is LYING FUCKING VERMIN JEW. Changed name from Minschbaum. Shitsbaum. BRING DOWN THE FUCKING HAMMER on his lyin' kike ass!! 14/88

Report: More than 10,000 children in three Central American countries have starved to death over last year as drought enters 10th year. U.S. sends more troops to Southern Border War front.

Holland's people are JEWS MUSLIMS various exotic sexual groups BLACK church ladies college QUEERS ... they all hate white men. HATE them back. HEIL HAMMER!!

Wildfires jump lines, grow to 2.5 million acres, 12,500 homes, businesses destroyed; downtown Los Angeles evacuated; Gov. Blanchard asks Pres. Holland for military assistance.

Hammer shit is lies FAKE NEWS. Ironheel.com is FAKE NEWS. Only way Hammer fucked boys was in Dem dreams. Truth @Thunderfront.com. BRING DOWN THE HAMMER!!!

Two students killed in crossfire as armed teacher, mass shooter engage in school hallway; death toll now at 15 as shooter flees.

Inclusive Violence IV shits and Holland/Deep State allies created fiction about Hammer and bomb and boys. Inclusive Violence real terrorist here. Sad. BRING DOWN THE HAMMER!

Savannah downtown under ten feet of water as Hurricane Xerxes hammers Georgia coast; late season storm leaves thousands dead in Carribbean.

I AM SO SICK OF NIGGERS, KIKES, GOOKS, QUEERS, SPICS, SAME SEX, MIXED RACE, ELITE SHITS. GUYS WORKING FOR JAP COMPANY DESERVED TO DIE. BRING DOWN THE HAMMER!

"The genius of the United States is not best or most in its executives or legislatures, nor in its ambassadors or authors or colleges, or churches, or parlors, nor even in its newspapers or inventors, but always most in the common people." @WaltWhitman got it oh so wrong.

(Room remains ghost-lit by multiple screens, silent with unbearable noise. Trammell stands perfectly still back to audience, as if at an altar of light, curtain closes very slowly.)

Hello, America. It's a beautiful day in the USA, isn't it? Or at least it's going to be. My name is Danielle Two, and I have news that isn't fake at all: If you are an American citizen who makes less than forty thousand dollars a year, then I have ten thousand dollars I'd like to give you. That's right. Give you. It's not quite that simple, but almost. Let me explain.

I represent the Dance for Democracy Foundation, a new nonprofit organization dedicated to a lost notion in America: The pursuit of happiness. Started by the leaders of our nation's premier information companies, Dance for Democracy is dedicated to making the lives of forgotten Americans better – happier – through annual grants of five thousand or ten thousand dollars.

All you have to do is dance. That's right, dance. Here's how it works: America's leading information providers – Artichoke, Googly, Faceface, Impetus and Microsquish – will send out notifications to millions of users who are struggling financially throughout the year. You won't know when you'll be picked, so you'll want to stay connected 24/7. You might be eligible for the $10,000 grant two or even three times per year, depending on your income and situation.

One thing you need to know: There is an automatic disqualifier. The pursuit of happiness can't tolerate hate. So to qualify for your Dance for Democracy grant, you must drop your membership in TRIBE, IV and other organizations that promote hate. With money in your pocket and your family in better shape, you won't have time for hate anyway, will you? You'll be part of the Dance for Democracy team!

Here's how it works. At some point – could be today, could be a month from now, could be both! – You'll hear a quick phrase on your phone, Thoughtext reader, headfeed or other device, that sounds like this: Let's Dance! Then an old song your parents or grandparents may have listened to will start playing, a catchy little tune that will get your toe tapping, and all you have to do is walk outside your house and start shaking your bootie. Then take a selfie video of yourself doing it or have your spouse or a friend take it, follow the eligibility rules in the notification, and send it on to Dance for Democracy. You'll have to include a few documents such as proof of income and household status, but after that, a check for $5,000 will be deposited in your account! And here's the kicker: Because we want America to be a happier place for everyone, if you dance with a person of a different race, we'll double your grant and give you $10,000!

So stay plugged in, America, and let's all Dance for Democracy!

(Offer-not-valid-in-Puerto-Rico-Guam-and-American-Samoa-Grant-awards-are-subject-to-federal-and-state-taxes-where-applicable-Members-of-TRIBE-(Take-Racial-Identity-Back-Evermore)-and-IV-(Inclusive-Violence)-and-certain-other-designated-political-hate-organizations-not-eligible-until-membership-is-dropped-Certain-other-eligibility-rules-apply-Dance-for-Democracy-Foundation-Inc.-is-a-nonprofit-organization-registered-in-Delaware.)

CHAPTER BREAKING

Alright, students, our time is almost up. We've covered a lot of ground, and I'd like to close the workshop with a look at today's breaking news. I trust you have kept your phones and headfeeds turned off during the workshop, as required for you to receive credit for the class, and I ask that you leave them turned off. You can certainly check Impetus, Thoughtext, Faceface, Googly, Artichoke, Twitwit, whatever your normal source for news may be, once the workshop is over, but for now, let's look at legitimate news. Here are the top stories today from Truth Network:

"The top advisor to presidential frontrunner Daniel Hammerschmidt said today that the candidate was directly involved in the planning of this morning's bombing of a Japanese cargo ship in Jacksonville that resulted in the deaths of four American workers.

"A spokesman for the FBI confirmed that investigators are exploring several potential scenarios in what they have called "an act of terrorism" but would not confirm or deny that Hammerschmidt is a suspect.

"Hammerschmidt called the allegation by TRIBE president and campaign advisor Dick Maestro "a complete fabrication" and "the ravings of a lunatic who used to be my friend." Hammerschmidt said he was "horrified" by the bombing and wanted nothing more than to find out who did it and bring him or her to justice."

And this, today's other top story:

"Presidential frontrunner Daniel Hammerschmidt has been accused of sexually assaulting young boys, including some as young as three years old, in a lawsuit filed by the boys' families in federal court.

"Hammerschmidt, still reeling from earlier accusations that he was involved in the Jacksonville port bombing Saturday morning, said in a Thoughtext message the lawsuit was "Total FAKE NEWS" and that the families were being paid by President Cassandra Holland's re-election campaign."

So-o-o-o. There you have it. It's been quite a busy news day, hasn't it? Tell me what you think in the interface section.

"Holy shit."

"Jesus Christ."

"This is all lies, man, all fucking lies from the mainstream media."

"Truth Network and the FBI are working for rich bitch nigger Holland's Deep State."

"I believe Hammerschmidt. Bring down the Hammer on Truth Network, FBI, all of them."

"Hold on, TRIBE shit. IV member here. Maybe you should believe your own dumbshit eyes. Check out the video on ironheel.com. Hammerschmidt is fucking a little boy, like, a baby, screaming in pain, and Hammerschmidt's dick is like two inches long!"

Alright, students, that's enough. We're shutting down comments for now. Instead let's talk about what we've just seen. How can we assess whether either of these news stories is true? Now, the video might seem to lend credibility to the lawsuit story, but videos can be altered, and you'll notice Truth Network didn't run it because it wasn't verified. Ironheel.com puts anything up. Also, anyone can file a lawsuit. We would need more information, but the bottom line on this story, at this early stage, is that we can't possibly know if it's true. Sometimes that's what news is: history as it happens, or doesn't happen. There is no perfect truth in news. Same can be said of the story on the bombing and Hammerschmidt's role. Investigators aren't saying yet, so we have only the word of an advisor who may have any number of motives to undermine the candidate's chances. That's why –

All of the student links go dark. No one is listening to Professor Ibid anymore. They have turned their devices back on. Class is over. Everyone is outside dancing.

CHAPTER FAULKNER

Li is a fish. The Colonel is a fish. Donnie and Baby are starfishes.

CHAPTER HONOR

Cassandra emerges from her tent. Niko the Rottweiler stays inside at her command. Her face is beauty broken. Katrina did not do this to her. God did not do this to her. One man did this to her. A second man did this to her. She has lost one eye, now covered by scarred stitched bumpy brown skin. She is beautiful. Harold gets up from the crate and hugs her long, awkwardly. He whispers to her "I will help you again, Cassandra, after I get through all this and get my wife and life back on track." Cassandra tells him no, he doesn't have to do that, she doesn't need anyone anymore, she can take care of herself. Lucy takes a photo she may or may not use. Cassandra holds her hand over her face after the click. And then from the remaining lid a single tear escapes. Lucy looks at her and feels universal love the kind that lives within floating inside embedded in a stranger.

"I won't tell your story if you don't want me too, Cassandra. I won't use the photo, either. It's your call. Totally your call. Old school journalistic honor."

"Thank you."

"How's my baby girl? Did you get your story?"

"I did and then some. I'm back with a vengeance, Mom, and I've got to file right away so I've only got a minute or so to talk."

"Go."

"I just needed to know something. How did you fall in love with Dad? How did you fall in love with a white guy? It wasn't really normal when you were 19 or 20. At least where you grew up."

"Back in the time of the elders, huh? Yeh, it was kind of weird, I guess. None of my friends dated a white guy. But weird feels normal when it's true. Normal is what's weird because it's false, everything around you and what you're supposed to be instead of you. Me and your dad were just, we fell in love like anyone does, I guess. Something clicked, something in the eyes. His eyes smiled, those blue eyes smiled, with a little sexy mischief. Like we were the only ones in on a joke. That's what it was. I had to remember a little. At a concert, someone we just met said the band on stage was great, and without saying a word, your dad and me knew they were horrible. I guess that's when I fell in love, or at least the first spark of love. A crappy band created you."

"That's funny. Do you still miss him?"

"Every minute except when I'm concentrating on work or something else. But always when I'm alone. And I don't mind it. I mind the other, though. The guy is still sitting on Death Row, watching TV, using a computer, living and breathing. I still see his eyes in the courtroom. The stupidness, the empty stupid nothing behind them, arrogance somehow from that, an empty skull, empty hate, no reason, your father kissed me on a sidewalk for God's sake, no reason, no reason, TRIBE motherfucker-motherfucker-motherfucker."

"Mom, stop. Stop. I'm so sorry. I am so so sorry. Please stop. Think about Dad at the concert. Think about you and me and Dad at the pool. Think about love, how much we loved each other. I hate the guy too, but nothing ever gets better that way. At least not for me."

"Me neither."

"Things do get better sometimes though when I miss Dad, and I don't mind missing him in that way, too, the good stuff, just like you said. We can't let it veer off to the other or we'll be destroyed. The task in front of you, Mom. For Dad's sake. I only brought him up because I met someone today I might love and it's kind of weird and different. I don't know. Maybe I've always leaned this way. But it might be just that I want to protect her, don't want her to be hurt anymore. It's kind of like something washed over me."

"I wish you hadn't brought him up, either. Now I've got to calm all down. You've made me sad all of a sudden and angry and I was having a pretty good day. My philosophy doesn't always work so well. Now what is it you said? Did I hear you say her? "

"Yes. Maybe. We'll see. I might not ever see her again. She's been through a lot and doesn't trust people much anymore."

"Well, make a point to see her again if you feel it, sweetheart. Just don't get caught up with someone so battered and ruined that they ruin you. I trust you. And don't bring up missing dad again anytime soon. Makes me crazy and wrong. Just when we're together, maybe, and not on the phone. I always love you, though."

"I know, Mom. I won't. I'm sorry. I always love you, too. I love him always too. We both love him always. Gotta file my story. Bye, Mom."

CHAPTER LOVE

Trammell heads home driving below the speed limit like an old man, his mind alive his soul exhausted. Nothing quite registers properly anymore. He should be easing down from the adrenaline and satisfied with self after the day just past and being part of a great story again after so many years but instead burrows burrows. An image crystallized from long ago quite suddenly brings sad helpless pain. Close to a plummet, might need to pull over. He keeps driving. He feels protected in his little rusted car and that thought leads to others distant and intimate. The plummet subsides. Back where he belongs: thoughts and notions and words within.

He drives the Toyota because it is well-made with interesting lines, sturdy even with its age, unlike his parents Ted and Sue Trammell, both dead now, who hated Japanese cars and only drove American-made ones because of Pearl Harbor, their generation's childhood horror, except for one little European foray with a Fiat, a detour away from the USA that Ted vowed never to take again. After the Fiat: Ford, Ford, Ford, Ford, Ford, Ford, Lincoln, the latter wrapping things up with a bit more luxury during Ted and Sue's country club retirement years in suburban Atlanta, their gated reward for Ted's post-World War II white college white housing white hiring and a lifetime of hard work as an engineer who made the most of being white, plowing forward with a smart professional mind and a constricted cultural mind that would not expand. Trammell and his brother never wanted for anything in their lives except modern thought and meaningful conversation.

"So, Dad," a teenaged Trammell asked the day after his father bought the Fiat, "you're willing to buy a car from a country that was a close friend of Hitler's but not from the Japanese who have now become one of our closest allies?"

Sue answered for her husband after Ted said simply, "That's right."

"The people in Italy," Sue explained, "are like us."

"But they helped Hitler murder six million Jews and gypsies and gay guys," the astounded 15-year-old responded. "Why wouldn't you take a stand against them?

"It's different," said Sue, "it's just different."

"And I've also done the homework and everything I've read says Fiats are very good cars, better than the Japanese cars," added Ted, trying to make pragmatism the central argument. "The 4-cylinder engine is sound."

As often happened, the teenage Trammell gave up quickly and retreated into his mind and its desire to live among free-thinking modern people. This, he never did. He has always lived in the United States.

Trammell keeps driving slowly toward home in the drift of irrelevant memories.

On several occasions as he finished high school, he helped his dad change the oil in the Fiat, something he could not give a shit about but did anyway so his dad would think they were bonding. They never did, but had a little moment once when they were changing the Fiat's oil. Ted grew to hate the little car, and when a stripped bolt fell into the oil pan Trammell heard "Shit!" whispered against the metal undercarriage, and it made him snicker. His dad apologized and Trammell said "No problem, dad, I hear it every day," "Not from me, you don't" and sure enough Trammell never heard it again, often wishing he would, wishing his dad would be a real person instead of a self-contained framework of white society, white government, white Christian Sundays. Nothing inside except adherence to the framework, carried out with hollow charm and rigid measure. No abuse, never abuse, paid all bills, bought nice houses nice cars, sent him to college. Ted and Sue Trammell both died last year without even a near-tear from Trammell their son. No blame no anger much gratitude for things money can buy just no connection that grew more distant the older he got. They introduced into his developing mind Don't drive through Niggertown, You know he's Jewish, They're all Mexicans now, Orientals aren't like us. Ted and Sue were a category of humans always present moving backward, with strong convictions not their own, fixed souls affluent or poor reproducing themselves. Their progeny: One son who became their opposite, had no children, another son who became them, fathered new ones who became them again. Always through humankind, where are the someones who do not diminish hope. Hidden. One tear. Working alone in laboratories, in the last of the wild places, in front of computers, in front of canvases, in sanctuaries that know human truths. The everyones are always and everywhere, the Beast, the Blob, the Banal, followers of the philosopher Mediocrites, the backward and forward line, millions upon millions upon millions upon billions, never grew, never rose, never listened, never flew, never believed Copernicus, never felt Van Gogh, never crushed it, never lived naked, never believed beyond belief, never heard Jesus, never loved spiders, never valued beyond values, never listened to their minds, never looked beyond their front door, never lived beyond their white, never tried, never lived up to Steinbeck, just whispered angrily among themselves clocking in clocking out, multiplying, starting Roth IRAs, getting drunk, never drinking, sitting in pews, making money, never having money, getting stronger, keeping the chain unbroken, into the 21st century, waiting for someone new to lead them.

Karen enters through a screen door on the back porch of his consciousness.

"Still ranting, huh?"

"Of course. Hello. In fact, ranting more than ever, Miss Marples. Keeps me alive. Always has. Kind of like rage rage against the dying of the species. That's what you never understood, how I needed it, or at least never respected."

"I understood it completely, Trammell. It's just fifty years of it day in day out is enough. It doesn't accomplish anything. Humanity just kept getting worse. It got to be like living with Debbie Downer."

"I think of it more like a white-boy version of Cesar Chavez or Malcolm X."

"But you used to go on and on about everything and anything. I don't think Malcolm X ever railed about some chippy cashier mispronouncing his name."

"Symptomatic. The littlest things are symptomatic. The decline of standard English, of education, of caring about standard English."

"Yada yada yada, Trammellovitch. And since when am I Miss Marples?"

"I don't know. Made it up on the fly. You always figured out the killer before she did."

"Anyway, Carrot Nose, the point is, your parents weren't the cause of the decline of western civilization. They were boring, conventional, shallow, polite Southern racists."

"My point exactly. Symptomatic. It wasn't just them. It was all of them. The poor dumb ones and the rich smart ones."

"Right, affluent white Republicans and NASCAR types are two sides of the same coin. Not moving us forward. Got it. And you forgot about chippy now-now-now digital youngsters who can't put their phones down long enough to think or to vote, your other favorite targets. They're all holding us back. I get it."

"You can be so nasty, Tiger Lily. Not what I loved about you. But you are what I loved."

"Ditto. I'm leaving now."

"Not yet, Baby. Don't go yet. I want to tell you something I never told you. Something I saw maybe twenty years ago and never told you about because I knew you would have been horrified. But it's never left me and it even popped up again today, even with all the other stuff going on. Had another little plummet about a half hour ago driving home. Saw this raccoon from twenty years ago. Just as vivid now as then. His eyes. He was about to give up but not yet. And I was the reason he wasn't giving up. I was coming home then, too, on our street, and the raccoon had been hit, his entire back half crushed, and he was propped up on his front legs trying to go somewhere but couldn't, his lower half was crushed, and he looked at me directly in my eyes as I slowed down to see if I could help, and he was asking me for help. About to give up but not yet. Nothing he could do. Nothing I could do. None of it his fault. Human idiocy, some dumbshit driving too fast so he could be an insignificant dumbshit somewhere else."

"Or maybe he ran out in front of someone who couldn't do anything and felt terrible about it. Everyone is not a dumbshit, Trammell, despite appearances. Ease away. He's not suffering anymore. He's not. I know he's not. He was then but he's not now. You need to think about small beauty. Walk down a dirt road, see a small farm and stop walking and just look, the red wheelbarrow glazed with rainwater beside the white chickens. Think about your small beauty.

"You know Williams now?"

"Yes, I know all your poetry crap now."

"It's not crap."

"I know that too.

"Well aren't you something. Maybe I'll be enlightened more on your ways when I've moved on. I'll understand the deeper meaning of nagging."

"Screw you, Trammell. Creating a home that comforts and keeps you is small beauty."

"Yes it is, Wise Maiden. With a little leeway, of course, on the kitchen counter crumbs. You know some people didn't even think that was a poem. So much depends on these small moments, your own little world of small beauty, and then Williams proved it by creating one of those moments in 16 words. On a prescription pad, no less. That's what a poem is, for God's sake. How did you know I used that sometimes for my plummets?"

"Well, I just do, Carlos Magee. It's pretty cool and knowing here. Now go inside and see Norman. He's been waiting all day for you. Kiss him for me and tell him I love him. Ease away."

"I will. I've already shaken it pretty much. I always do. You helped. Thank you, Babaloo. You seem to be able to handle animal suffering better now too. You couldn't even watch nature documentaries with me before."

"Not better, just broader. Big picture. A part of me cries all the time, but it's only a part. Dickens got it right. Best and worst always co-exist. Always have, always will. Even here. We'll never get it right. The someones will just have to keep trying. As you call them. So go go go and don't plummet, Trammell, and cool down the raging pop philosophy crap before you see Norman. He doesn't like loud voices."

"He's completely deaf now and actually likes my rants, thank you very much. He remembers them from when he could hear. I can tell. They give him comfort, I'm pretty sure."

"If that's what you want to believe, Trammell. Bye."

"Bye."

An old man smiles driving alone in his car.

He got his love of reading and songbirds from mother Sue. He got thoroughness and precision from father Ted. He loves them institutionally without tears.

Trammell pulls into his driveway and upon shutting down and staring comfortably at nothing comes to realize there has been music playing outside his closed windows during much of the trip, and he thought he saw Rob Cantsitstill dancing in the driveway next door. The fog has risen higher than the trees and now encloses everything. It is either real or fake or both does not matter.

CHAPTER WORLD

Nothing is true. This is the end of the story for Norman. If two living things and their belief in each other cannot be trusted then nothing can be trusted. Trammell has not come back and night has descended upon the forest outside the sliding glass doors. Norman cannot turn on the floodlight like Trammell always does and so he can only see murky fog and black forest beyond his own reflection. Trammell left the inside light on for him and Norman can only see himself on the floor and the family room all around him with the sofa where Trammell should be sitting watching TV with Norman beside him sleeping on the newspaper he is trying to read. Nothing is as it should be at this time in this world in this reflection. The scary fog on the ground has gotten bigger and closer and now licks the sliding glass door just on the other side of his reflection, and the little pieces of black movement brush against the glass. The black movement at least is not inside. Still scary. Think elsewhere. Think about if things were true. A normal night, a movie on television, Trammell ranting at the movie when it is interrupted by The Making Of... two camera-ready hipsters making certain that we fully understand and are constantly aware that everything we are looking at is fake. The director talks about CG battle scenes. The actors talk about their preparation for the role. The movie then returns and promos wiggle in and out of the corner as a soldier dies. Keep it fake, baby, make it all shrapnel, Trammell will say. We want you to know with absolute certainty that everything is fake. We want you to tweet and check Faceface and send Thoughtexts during the movie and during dinner and in all situations two feet away from another person so that both of you are ghost-lit non-existent non-beings. We want you to do this continually, to be assured continually that flesh and voice and eyes and mind are fake. We want you to believe lies and send them to your friends and double down on them once you find out they are lies. We want you to trust and worship the people who are loudest and angriest. Be frightened and outraged by them and vote for them. We want you to find comfort and strength in contempt. We want you to be maligned and forgotten and find strength in victimhood. Believe that the world is going to hell. Believe that the world is Headfeed and Headfeed is the world and the only truth is within the helmet. We want you to be ghost-lit and self-involved. We want you young and old to do/be all of these things. The dwindling rest of us who live and breathe the planet's air freely are sad about it, but if it makes you happy we shall sink on your behalf. We have no choice, do we? The prophets of The Dumb will always prevail.

Trammell shuts up in remembered rant and Norman's old brain awakens to the real. He does not hear but feels the rumble of the front door opening, smells cigarette smoke oozing from pores and trots on old legs happily down the hallway.

Toward love.

"Hey, big man. I missed you too. Karen does, too, and still loves you very much. She wants a kiss, but I'll have to sit down to do it. My back is blown. We missed our workout and stretches today, didn't we. Come here. You smell good for an old man. Big day today.

Very weird day. Your dad was involved with some bigtime shit and a great story. I actually saved America, Norman, if you can believe that. Something, a joke really, I said years ago and it became an evil scheme. The good side of evil, I suppose. The racist clown won't be elected Tuesday, so I guess you'd have to say four deaths were worth it. That sounds pretty cold, doesn't it. Of course, they probably weren't worth it, nothing will be saved, but it sounds good to say your Dad saved America, doesn't it. I'll tell you and Karen about it all later. We'll stay up and watch some TV."

Toward truth.

"Believe it or not, we still need to get out the newsletter. You up for it? I'm tired, too, but it shouldn't take long. Pretty easy day on the local fake front. National's the one that's crazy. We'll get a little supper before we start, if I can grind myself up eventually."

Toward hope.

"I think Lucy and James are going to be able to nail this bastard Maestro. Or savior Maestro, depending on your perspective. Either way, they'll get him. I gladly turn it over to them. They remind me of me, a long time ago. They're getting help from one of Maestro's aides and a surveillance guy who sent Lucy a file and from a homeless IT guy, believe it or not. There are someones out there, Norman. Very hard to find, but that's all we've got, right? This Lucy girl is a someone, Norman. Lovely Lucy. That rarest of things, a young person of objectivity and quiet thought."

Toward hidden.

"I kind of like the fog now, don't you? Hated it, and I know you hate it too, but tonight I kind of like it. Real or fake, who cares, right, Norman? No one will be able to see us at all."

Toward wonder.

"I wonder where The Colonel is. What he sees. What he knows. Wonder if Li is there. That was his wife. He loved her, I think, as much as me and you loved Karen. Love Karen. Wonder if he's in the same place as Donnie and Baby. Wonder if he's anywhere at all. Or everywhere at once. The oversoul is an interesting notion, Emerson's take on Hinduism I think, reincarnation on the molecular level but universal at the same time, the molecules converting to some kind of ethereal energy, quarks in the quiet night, landing somewhere, landing everywhere, inhabiting something close to those who know them and love them, sort of what we believe about Karen, isn't it, Norman. The bromeliad blooms are her, and that rock with the red vein is her, too. All we need, right? The rest is lost, Norman. Forget it. Let 'em crash and burn. Good thing we'll be gone. What do you think it will be. Some kind of bizarre blend of Soylent Green and Mad Max and Waterworld? Costner got screwed on that, didn't he? The Postman, too. Something so simple as a letter can save us. Both of them prescient. Maybe a little preachy, maybe a little too long, but prescient. Anyway, Norman, whatever happens, there will always be old men and cats like us, right? All we need. Our own little world."

Toward dance.

"Something strange on the way home, buddy. That old song we like by Paul Simon was playing on some of the scrollboxes. I know you didn't hear it, but it was strange. I was kind of distracted, had one of my rants about my parents and humanity, and I talked to Karen a little bit, she's doing okay, but I'm pretty sure also that every street I drove down on the way home, that song was playing at, like, every other house. And people were out dancing to it. When I was pulling in I saw our idiot neighbor Rob out on his driveway dancing to it. Bundled Wire Man tripping the light. Weird. Great song, though. The one with the pennywhistle flute and the bass run. The toe just naturally taps. The lyrics sort of fit us, don't they Norman. You're my little bodyguard and I'm your goofy long lost pal. It will always be so, squire. Something true you can count on. Come here, let me hold you. I'll sing the song in your ear so you can feel the vibrations. Can we still dance when we can't stand up? A question for the ages. Of course we can. Let us sing and dance in the hallway of our home, Sir Norman!"

Toward

About the Author

Cal Massey is a retired newspaper editor who is not an enemy of the people. He won numerous state and national awards for news that was not fake. He and his wife Lynn and six cats live in their own little world in Florida. This is his first novel at age 65.

A Checklist of JEF Titles

*** Winners of the Kenneth Patchen Award for the Innovative Novel**

- ☐ **0** ***Projections*** **by Eckhard Gerdes**
- ☐ **2** ***Ring in a River*** **by Eckhard Gerdes**
- ☐ **3** ***The Darkness Starts Up Where You Stand*** **by Arthur Winfield Knight**
- ☐ **4** ***Belighted Fiction***
- ☐ **5** ***Othello Blues*** **by Harold Jaffe**
- ☐ **9** ***Recto & Verso: A Work of Asemism and Pareidolia*** **by Dominic Ward & Eckhard Gerdes (Fridge Magnet Edition)**
- ☐ **9B** ***Recto & Verso: A Work of Asemism and Pareidolia*** **by Dominic Ward & Eckhard Gerdes (Trade Edition)**
- ☐ **11** ***Sore Eel Cheese*** **by The Flakxus Group (Limited Edition of 25)**
- ☐ **14** ***Writing Pictures: Case Studies in Photographic Criticism 1983-2012*** **by James R. Hugunin**
- ☐ **15** ***Wreck and Ruin: Photography, Temporality, and World (Dis)order*** **by James R. Hugunin**
- ☐ **17** ***John Barth, Bearded Bards & Splitting Hairs***
- ☐ **18** ***99 Waves*** **by Persis Gerdes**
- ☐ **23** ***The Laugh that Laughs at the Laugh: Writing from and about the Pen Man, Raymond Federman***
- ☐ **24** ***A-Way with it!: Contemporary Innovative Fiction***
- ☐ **28** ***Paris 60*** **by Harold Jaffe**
- ☐ **29** ***The Literary Terrorism of Harold Jaffe***
- ☐ **33** ***Apostrophe/Parenthesis*** **by Frederick Mark Kramer**
- ☐ **34** ***Journal of Experimental Fiction 34: Foremost Fiction: A Report from the Front Lines***
- ☐ **35** ***Journal of Experimental Fiction 35***
- ☐ **36** ***Scuff Mud*** **(cd)**
- ☐ **37** ***Bizarro Fiction: Journal of Experimental Fiction 37***
- ☐ **38** ***ATTOHO #1*** **(cd-r)**
- ☐ **39** ***Journal of Experimental Fiction 39***
- ☐ **40** ***Ambiguity*** **by Frederick Mark Kramer**
- ☐ **41** ***Prism and Graded Monotony*** **by Dominic Ward**
- ☐ **42** ***Short Tails*** **by Yuriy Tarnawsky**
- ☐ **43** ***Something Is Crook in Middlebrook*** **by James R. Hugunin**
- ☐ **44** ***Xanthous Mermaid Mechanics*** **by Brion Poloncic**
- ☐ **45** ***OD: Docufictions*** **by Harold Jaffe**
- ☐ **46** ***How to Break Article Noun*** **by Carolyn Chun***
- ☐ **47** ***Collected Stort Shories*** **by Eric Belgum**
- ☐ **48** ***What Is Art?*** **by Norman Conquest**
- ☐ **49** ***Don't Sing Aloha When I Go*** **by Robert Casella**
- ☐ **50** ***Journal of Experimental Fiction 50***
- ☐ **51** ***Oppression for the Heaven of It*** **by Moore Bowen***
- ☐ **52** ***Elder Physics*** **by James R. Hugunin**
- ☐ **53.1** ***Like Blood in Water: Five Mininovels (The Placebo Effect Trilogy #1)*** **by Yuriy Tarnawsky**

☐ 53.2 *The Future of Giraffes: Five Mininovels (The Placebo Effect Trilogy #2)* by Yuriy Tarnawsky
☐ 53.3 *View of Delft: Five Mininovels (The Placebo Effect Trilogy #3)* by Yuriy Tarnawsky
☐ 54 *You Are Make Very Important Bathtime* by David Moscovich
☐ 55 *Minnows: A Shattered Novel* by Jønathan Lyons
☐ 56 *Meanwhile* by Frederick Mark Kramer
☐ 58A *Tar Spackled Banner* by James R. Hugunin
☐ 58B *Return to Circa '96* by Bob Sawatzki*
☐ 60 *Case X* by James R. Hugunin
☐ 61 *Naked Lunch at Tiffany's* by Derek Pell
☐ 62 *Tangled in Motion* by Jane L. Carman
☐ 64 *The Hunter* by Dominic Ward
☐ 65 *A Little Story about Maurice Ravel* by Conger Beasley, Jr.
☐ 66 *Psychedelic Everest* by Brion Poloncic
☐ 67 *Between the Legs* by Kate Horsley*
☐ 68 *Claim to Oblivion: Selected Essays and Interviews* by Yuriy Tarnawsky
☐ 69 *Passions and Shadows or Shadows and Passions* by Frederick Mark Kramer
☐ 70 *Afterimage: Critical Essays on Photography* by James R. Hugunin
☐ 71 *Goosestep* by Harold Jaffe
☐ 72 *Science Fiction: A Poem!* by Robin Wyatt Dunne
☐ 73 *Offbeat/Quirky*
☐ 74 *Mouth* by Charles Hood*
☐ 75 *Q↔A* by James R. Hugunin
☐ 76 *Literary Yoga* by Yuriy Tarnawsky
☐ 77 *Experimental Literature: A Collection of Statements* edited by Jeffrey R. Di Leo and Warren Motte
☐ 78 *The Skrat Prize Memorial Anthology* by R.M. Strauss*
☐ 79 *Black Scat Books: A Bibliography 2012 – 2018* compiled by Grace Murray
☐ 80 *Finding Mememo* by James R. Hugunin
☐ 81 *Porn-anti-Porn* by Harold Jaffe
☐ 82 *Understanding Franklin Thompson* by Jim Meirose
☐ 83 *Warm Arctic Nights* by Yuriy Tarnawsky
☐ 84 *The Iguanas of Heat* by Yuriy Tarnawsky
☐ 85 *Death at Half Mast* by Denis Emorine
☐ 86 *Those Brave As the Skate Is* by Patrick Keller*
☐ 87 *The Marble Corridor* by Ryan Madej
☐ 88 *Crocodile Smiles* by Yuriy Tarnawsky
☐ 89 *Plague City* by Genelle Chaconas*
☐ 90 *Picky Hunting* by James R. Hugunin
☐ 91 *"The Greatest Place on Earth": A Personal Note: A Work of Absurdity?* by Jeff Weisman
☐ 92 *Own Little Worlds* by Cal Massey*